Sally

Sally

(Original title: Three of a Kind)

by LOUISE DICKINSON RICH

Illustrated by William M. Hutchinson

SCHOLASTIC BOOK SERVICES
New York Toronto London Auckland Sydney Tokyo

ISBN: 0-590-09204-9

Copyright © 1970 by Louise Dickinson Rich. This edition is pub-
lished by Scholastic Book Services, a division of Scholastic Maga-
zines, Inc., by arrangement with Franklin Watts, Inc., publishers
of the book under the title THREE OF A KIND.

14 13 12 11 10 9 8 7 6 5   9/7 01/8

Printed in the U.S.A.

Sally

CHAPTER 1

Sally Gray awoke with a feeling in the back of her mind that something special was going to happen today. For a moment she could not think what it was. She lay there snug under the covers in the frosty little room, looking up at the slanted ceiling, listening to the surf breaking on the reefs beyond the harbor, trying to remember. The windows still showed black through their tiny panes, but she could hear Rhoda and Ben talking down in the kitchen, so it must be later than it seemed. The sun rose late and set early in January on Star Island, seven miles off the Maine coast. She had learned that in the months since the social workers, Miss Bridges and Miss Carr, had brought her and the other State Kids to their new foster homes in Starhaven.

Today was Saturday, which meant no school. That was special. Not that she minded school all that much. School here was different from school over on the main, as the islanders called the mainland. Living as she had in so many different foster homes, she must have attended a dozen schools back there, she thought. They had all been big and modern, with visual aids, social studies, and physical education classes. Here there was only one teacher, Miss Mills, for all the grades. She stuck pretty much to reading, writing, and arithmetic, with a little history and geography thrown in. The whole school had only eleven pupils—the eight State Kids and the three island children. It was a little one-room school that had come very near to being no school at all. The state had almost closed it. A school of three was too small to receive the state aid necessary to support it. Starhaven, like so many Maine island villages, was slowly shrinking as its young people left it for the better opportunities of the mainland.

Then somebody had thought of making it a big enough school by asking the Child Welfare Department to place a group of homeless children with island families. So here they were—she and Tom and Larry and the rest—living out in the middle of the ocean in the best foster homes any of them had ever had. She, Sally, wasn't going to complain about any school that was the reason for her being here with Ben and Rhoda Cooper, that was for sure.

But what was it about today? It was something besides Saturday—something out of the ordinary. Gathering her courage, Sally flung back the bedclothes, jumped out of bed, and slammed down the window against the flow of cold air that smelled of the sea and of fir trees. As she turned, shivering a little, to reach for her clothes, she saw the neatly wrapped package on her bureau.

❧ 4

Of course! What a birdbrain she was! Today was Rhoda's birthday. She ought to have remembered that, considering all the trouble she had gone to over Rhoda's present. She had wanted to get something nice, but she'd only had fourteen cents to her name. Ben would have given her some money, under the circumstances, but she wanted the present to be from her, and her alone. So she had made a deal with Bert Elder, the storekeeper. She had swept out the store every day after school for a week in exchange for a pretty little cut-glass pickle dish that she had seen Rhoda pick up, admire, and regretfully put down again. Bert had thrown in a piece of birthday wrapping paper and a length of blue ribbon because, he said, he admired her enterprise.

Now she dressed quickly in her Saturday clothes—warm slacks, plaid shirt, and wool sweater. Then she threw the blankets back over the foot of the bed—Rhoda was fussy about airing beds—picked up the package, and raced downstairs.

As always on winter mornings, the kitchen was warm and bright in the soft light of the kerosene lamps, and fragrant with the odor of bacon and toast. Rhoda was drinking a cup of coffee. She smiled at Sally, her thin, dark face lighting up under her crest of graying hair.

"Ben's shaving," she said, "but he'll be through by the time you've washed and are ready to comb your hair."

"Shaving?" Ben, like all the other island men, was a lobsterman. In winter none of them shaved before going out on the icy seas to haul their lobster traps. That was, they said, an easy way to get your face frozen. "Oh, of course. He won't be going out to haul today."

Instead, Sally knew, Ben would be going over to Stillport on the mainland to meet the Coopers' oldest son, Nathan, and his wife and three children. They were coming to Star Island to celebrate Rhoda's birthday. Because Nathan's job had kept him in California, this was to be their first visit in over four years. Ben and Rhoda had been looking forward to it for weeks, and so had Sally.

"Happy birthday, Rhoda!" Sally extended the package a little shyly.

"A present for me? Now that was real thoughtful of you!" Rhoda carefully untied the ribbon and rolled it smoothly around her fingers. Then she unwrapped the gift, folding the pretty paper neatly. "Oh, Sally! I've been admiring this down to Bert's—I do thank you!"

Sally worked the handle of the pump vigorously and splashed icy water onto her face. "I'm glad you like it," she said through the muffling folds of the rough towel.

"This is going to be a great birthday for me, all right," Rhoda went on. "I'll bet those grandchildren of mine have grown out of all recognition. I can hardly wait—"

She had put the pickle dish aside and apparently forgotten it. All her thoughts were plainly on the arrival of her son and his children. Oh, well, Sally thought, she really did like my present. I don't expect her to do cartwheels over it. I guess her own family is a lot more im-

portant to her than any old glass dish. That's only natural.

"The coast's clear in here," Ben called from the little room in back of the chimney. Although people on Star Island had to wash at their kitchen sinks, Rhoda would not let anyone shave or comb their hair there. She said it was unsanitary.

Ben's big bulk filled the door. "You'd save yourself a lot of time and trouble if you'd let me take the scissors to those pigtails, Sally," he said. " 'Twouldn't take more'n a minute."

"No!" Sally sounded more abrupt than she intended. But nobody, not even Ben, was going to cut off her hair.

"Why not? Short hair's a sight easier—"

Sally smiled at him in what she hoped was a mysterious manner. "I've got my reasons," she told him.

She did have, too, although nothing would induce her to give them. Spoken out loud, they would sound too silly and maybe too conceited. Long ago, when she was staying temporarily at one of the shelters the state maintained for unwanted children who were waiting to be assigned to foster homes, she had overheard two women visitors talking about her. Looking back, she was pretty sure that one of them had been interested in adopting a little girl. Probably they had not realized how much small children understand, especially those who are at the mercy of the world. You learned pretty fast, Sally knew, when you had no one but yourself to depend on.

❧ 8

One of the women had said, "But she's such a homely little thing."

The other had nodded. Then she had said, "Except for that glorious red-gold hair. It's her redeeming feature."

Neither of the women had adopted Sally, and no one else had, either. So, for all her eleven years, she had been shifted about from home to home until she had landed here on Star Island. But she had never forgotten that remark about her hair. So, all right; she was too tall for her age and skinny and freckled, and her mouth was too big and she had green cat's-eyes; but her hair was pretty, and no one was going to cut it off. Plenty of people had tried, using Ben's arguments about wasted time and trouble, but she had stopped them. At first, she had kicked and screamed and clawed and scratched at the sight of scissors. Later, she had learned to braid her hair herself, and from then on anybody who didn't like it could just lump it.

Ben had left by the time Sally came back into the kitchen, and Rhoda was placing Sally's plate of bacon and scrambled eggs on the table. On the island, everybody ate and practically lived in their big, pleasant kitchens.

"Eat up lively while it's hot," Rhoda urged. "I'll have myself another cup of coffee to keep you company." She sat down opposite Sally and sighed contentedly. "Fifty-five today. My, I don't know where the time has gone.

It seems like only yesterday that Nathan was sitting in that very chair you're sitting in now, with his chin just clearing the table, and the other two were toddling around underfoot. Now Albert's in Texas, and Steve's somewhere on the other side of the world with the Navy, and Nathan's got children of his own bigger'n he was then."

"Aren't Steve and Albert married?" Sally knew the answer, but she could see that Rhoda was enjoying talking about her family.

"Not yet, but there's plenty of time. What I *hope*—" Rhoda turned her coffee cup a little restlessly. "What I *hope* is that they'll come home and marry girls from around here that I can feel easy with. Ben and I always wanted a daughter, but it wasn't to be, so we made the best of it. Not that I'm complaining." She smiled. "Three better boys than ours never drew breath."

Sally could believe it, if they were anything like their parents.

"Still, I always hankered to have a girl around the house. That's why, when it was decided to bring you state wards over from the main, we asked especially if we could have a girl. Best bargain we ever made, that I'll take oath to."

"Pretty nice deal for me, too," Sally assured her sincerely. "I never had it so good in all my life."

"All your life!" Rhoda chuckled. "Wait till you're fifty-five." Then she sobered. "Everything was different here when I was growing up. Then folks stayed put on the island. They were born here and grew up here and married other islanders. They started their own families right here. They didn't go skyhooting off to the main, soon as they were out of knee breeches, getting educations and highfalutin jobs and marrying strange girls with off-island ways and notions. If a woman like me didn't have a daughter of her own, she could count on having a daughter-in-law that she'd always known and liked and understood, living right here in the village, and that was the next-best thing."

"Don't you like Nathan's wife?" Sally wasn't sure she should ask, but Rhoda had almost invited the question.

Rhoda swept the silverware lying by her place into a pile with a small clatter. "I *try* to like her," she said, rather fiercely. Then her tone moderated. "Oh, not that I *dis*like Laurel, you understand. It's just that she's— Well, not like us. She's a city girl—lived in New York all her life until she met Nathan at the university and married him right after graduation. The first time they visited us, she acted like she was in a foreign country where she didn't understand the language or the customs. Lord, she didn't know one end of a boat from the other."

Sally felt a sneaking sympathy for Laurel. She'd had her own troubles with the language and the customs when she'd first come here. It had taken her a while to get used to a whole village of men who went to work not when the clock said it was time, but when the tide served right, as they said. She remembered how puzzled she'd been on her first rainy day when Rhoda had told her she'd better oil up. She had simply been advising Sally to put on an oilskin raincoat.

"Oh, she learned fast," Rhoda went on. "Laurel's smart as a whip, that I'll say for her. She's pleasant, too, and ambitious for Nathan. I believe this transfer to Boston that he'd hoped for, but not really expected, is partly Laurel's doing. Nathan plugs along doing his job the best he's able, and cal'lates that's enough. But that's not enough for Laurel. She knows the right way to butter up the right people, and that helps, I guess. Oh, I'll not deny she's a good wife to Nathan. I'll give credit where credit's due."

"A good wife, but not a good daughter-in-law?" Sally asked.

"Oh, I don't know." Rhoda made a fluttery gesture that was unlike her usual positive manner. "I can't really say that. She's always lovely to me. It's just that I can't get close to her. Even her name puts me off. It's fancified and outlandish. Laura, now, is a good plain name I could cotton to. But Laurel! Out here on the island, the only laurel we know is a bush that blossoms in the spring."

Privately, Sally thought that Laurel was a pretty name for a girl.

"I shouldn't run on to you like this, Sally," Rhoda apologized. "I don't know what got into me. I wouldn't for the world have Nathan know how I feel about his wife, so just forget the whole thing, will you?" She stood up quickly and started stacking the dirty dishes. "Great Heavens, look at the time! We've got to flax round some, if we're going to get this place put to rights before it's time to go down and meet the folks. I plan to be standing right there on the edge of the wharf when Ben comes into harbor. I can't wait to get my hands on them grand-children of mine, especially little Benjie. The two girls are precious, but Benjie— Well, he's our first grand-son, besides being his grandpa's namesake, so I suppose it's natural we set such store by him, even though we've never seen him. He was born after they went to California. I wouldn't have the others guess it for anything, but just between the two of us, I'll have to admit that we're partial to Benjie."

CHAPTER 2

The sun was well up when Sally and Rhoda left the house to go down to the harbor. The sea to the east was a blinding shimmer of gold, and to the west, a restless expanse of deep blue. The mainland smudged the far horizon darkly. Over there was Stillport, the coastal city that served as the islanders' shopping center. Twice a week the ferry came over from Stillport, bringing the mail, supplies, and the rare visitors. But Saturday was not ferry day, so Ben had gone across in his own lobster boat to bring back his son's family. They had driven down from Boston during the night.

"I'm glad we've got a good day for them," Rhoda said with satisfaction. She looked to right and left at the neat little houses lining the steep dirt road, Starhaven's main and only street. She reminded Sally of a good housewife making sure that her home was in perfect order. "Take a good bright day like this, with a little sugar-dusting of snow on the ground, and I don't believe there's a prettier place in the world than right here. When company comes, I like Star Island to put its best foot forward."

Sally agreed. In the year and a half that she had lived here, she had grown to love the island more than any other place she had been. She found herself, like Rhoda, checking the appearance of the village.

Up the hill in front of the Chandlers' house their big black dog, Mate, was idly nosing around the yard. That meant that the three bigger boys on the island were out hauling—Matt Cole with his father; Tom and Larry, the two state boys, with their foster fathers. Otherwise, Mate would be with them. Farther down the road, Linda Allen was hanging dish towels on a line in back of her house. Linda was Sally's best friend, one of the local children and the only girl of Sally's age on the island.

Sally whistled through her front teeth, a piercing sound of which she was secretly proud, and waved when Linda turned. "See you later," she called, and Linda answered something about having to help her mother this morning. Sally waved again and went back to her inspection of the village.

The houses looked pretty, each with its plume of woodsmoke rising from the chimney. Now that she was used to it, she rather liked to see roofs without TV antennas sticking up from them. Nobody on Star Island had television. Nobody had a telephone or car, either. The light snow on the road was marred only by footprints—all headed down to the harbor—left by the men who had gone out hauling before dawn. In front of the store at the foot of the hill, two women were talking with Bert Elder, the storekeeper. They laughed at something he said and started up the road.

Sally gave a last look all around—at the trim houses, at the pointed fir trees growing thick above the village against the blue sky, at the bright sea encircling everything. Rhoda was right, she concluded. This might well be the prettiest place in the world.

"There's Ben now, right outside harbor," Rhoda said, and quickened her step. It still surprised Sally, after all this time, to see how unerringly each island woman could pick out her husband's boat, no matter how far away it was or how many others were in sight. "We'll get there in good season, like I wanted," Rhoda went on.

Ben's boat was just coming out of the narrow channel between the open sea and the harbor when Sally and Rhoda arrived at the landing. The boat crossed the sheltered basin at lowered speed, sending a gentle wash under the long-legged wharfs and up onto the sloping pebble beach.

"There they are!" Rhoda exclaimed. "Just look at them! Aren't they a sight for sore eyes?" She started waving frantically, and the people in the boat waved back. Catching the spirit of the occasion, Sally waved, too.

"There's Nathan," Rhoda said, "looking as natural as can be." She laughed a little. "No reason why he shouldn't, I s'pose. That's Laurel and the two girls— Tracy and Nan's their names. I don't see Benjie. They

❧ 16

must have sat him down back of the combing, where it's warm. Shows good sense, him not being used to this climate. He could easily catch a chill and—" She stopped and looked at Sally a little shyly. "How I do run on! You'll have to excuse me, Sally. It's just that I'm so happy and excited I don't know where I'm at."

Under Ben's expert hand the boat drew alongside the wharf in an easy, exact curve. Nathan, with a skill remembered from his island boyhood, tossed a mooring line over a post and knotted it securely. Then he stepped back and put one arm around his wife and the other around his two daughters. All together, in a manner clearly rehearsed, the four of them caroled, "Happy birthday to you—"

Standing in the background, Sally watched them singing and smiling so gaily. They looked like a picture-book family, she thought. In pictures, fathers were always tall and dark and handsome like Nathan, mothers were pretty and young and stylish like Laurel, and children were little blonde angels like Tracy and Nan. There was usually a boy; and, of course, there was Benjie, whom she couldn't yet see. Probably he was too young to have learned the birthday song. The Nathan Coopers were her idea of a perfect family, the family she had never had. There were even Grandfather and Grandmother, like in books, kindly and gentle and loving.

Although, actually, Ben didn't look so very gentle and kindly as he bent over the engine housing making some adjustment. He looked rather stern and serious. As Sally had learned during her months on the island, lobstermen were like that about their boats. Next to their families, their boats were the dearest things in their lives. Let a motor skip one little beat, and they acted as though the end of the world was in sight. That was undoubtedly the trouble with Ben now.

"Happy birthday, dear Grandma, happy birthday to you." The song came to an end, and Rhoda and Sally clapped loudly.

"That was lovely, and thank you," Rhoda said. "Now just hand me up my grandson. That'll be the happiest birthday present of all. I can't wait to see him—and to give my granddaughters each a big hug and kiss," she added as what Sally suspected was an afterthought. She remembered Rhoda's confession of her special feeling toward Benjie.

But the girls suspected nothing. They swarmed over the side of the boat onto the landing and flung themselves on their grandmother. The air was full of "My land, how you've grown!" and "I'm eight now and Nan's seven" and "We thought we'd never get here" and "How good it is to see you!"

Then Tracy said clearly, "Benjie couldn't come."

There was a sudden complete silence. Rhoda stared at Laurel. "You didn't bring Benjie?" she asked unbelievingly. "Why not? Is he sick? But of course he isn't," she reassured herself. "You'd never have left him if he was sick. I know that. I wouldn't have expected you to.

Nathan, answer me. Why didn't you bring Benjie? Ben, make him answer me."

Ben said rather heavily, "We'd best wait till we get home to talk about it, Rhody. It's a long story and I ain't sure I've got the rights of it yet myself."

Rhoda whirled on Laurel. "Tell me what's happened to him! At least I've got the right to know that."

Laurel put out a soothing hand. "Nothing's happened to him, Mother Cooper. He's just the same as always."

Sally looked at her sharply. It seemed an odd answer to her. Everybody said that she, Sally, was unusually smart about people, and she guessed that she was. You had to be, when you'd had to deal with strangers and their whims all your life. Right now she'd bet anything that Laurel was—well, maybe not out-and-out lying, but certainly hiding something. She could have said plainly, "Benjie's fine," and she hadn't.

Laurel bridged the awkward moment smoothly. "And this must be Sally whom we've heard so many nice things about."

Rhoda started and, with an effort, smiled. "Oh, dear. I forgot my manners. Yes, this is Sally." She made the introductions. "We'll go on up home," she concluded. "The men can come along as soon as they've snugged down the boat." She took Tracy's and Nan's hands in her own. "I've got some fresh gingerbread men all ready for my two favorite granddaughters, and we'll stir up some nice hot cocoa. You must be chilled through."

Good, Sally thought. Rhoda was back in charge of

herself. She was remembering that Nan and Tracy had probably looked forward to today, too. She was trying to make them feel welcome and wanted, in spite of her own disappointment. Good old Rhoda.

When the two men came up from the shore, the others were seated around the kitchen table with its red-and-white checked cloth, sipping hot drinks. Rhoda got up and poured coffee for Ben and Nathan, placing a square of warm gingerbread on each saucer. "This is just a snack to hold you until dinnertime," she said. She sat down and folded her hands in her lap. "Now let's stop beating around the bush. Where is Benjie?"

Nathan stirred his coffee, his eyes avoiding his mother's. "He's in a special school for children like him," he said quietly. "Benjie's—well, he isn't like normal children of his age. He's—slow."

Rhoda drew in her breath sharply. "Are you trying to tell me that Benjie's not—quite bright?" She looked suddenly older than her years.

"No!" Laurel's voice was emphatic. "We've had the best doctors anywhere and they all agree. There's nothing the matter with his mind or his body. The tests have proved that beyond a doubt."

"Then what is it?" Rhoda demanded.

"Nobody really knows," Nathan told her. "He's—they call it 'withdrawn.' He doesn't smile or talk or respond in any way, no matter how hard you try to reach him. He can see and hear all right. That isn't the trouble. It's as if he's shut up in himself, as if he's cut off from every-thing."

"The doctors have scientific names for it," Laurel said, "but Nathan has described it very well. He's—" She sighed.

"But there must be a reason. What caused it? There must be something they can do!"

"Nobody knows the reason. The best guess is some terrible shock early in life. Even the shock of being born, they say." Nathan sounded as though he didn't believe it, but had to accept it. "As for a cure, we've done every-thing—"

"Everything!" Laurel broke in. "Mother Cooper, be-lieve us, we've left no stone unturned."

"There." Ben spoke for the first time since he had come in. "Of course we believe that, Laurel. But a school now, away from his own folks. I don't cotton to that at all. It don't seem right."

"Father Cooper, it's the best thing. He'll be with chil-dren of his own sort. The people there are trained. They know about cases like Benjie, know what to do, what to expect, how to handle them."

Ben looked at her thoughtfully. "Maybe so. Maybe you're right. But I don't like the idea. Benjie isn't a *case* to be *handled* by strangers." He sounded scornful, un-like himself. "He's your and Nathan's son and he's our grandson. He's one of us, and we've always taken care of our own."

❦ 21

Sally almost cheered. She had been a case in the
Child Welfare Department files all her life, and she
knew what it was like not to be taken care of by someone who was her own.

"It isn't that simple," Laurel protested. "There's a lot
more involved than that." Her pretty face was flushed
and her blue eyes were almost angry.

Ben suddenly turned to Sally as if an echo of her
silent cheer had belatedly reached him, reminding him
of her and the other girls. "Why don't you and the girls

bundle up and take a tour of the island?" It sounded like a question, but it was a request. "Show them the sights, like?"

"I get the message," her eyes told him. Aloud she said heartily, "Good idea. I'll take them up through the woods to the cove, and back along the shore." That would give the Coopers plenty of time to thrash this thing out among themselves.

It was nice outdoors. The thin winter sunshine was warm, and there was no wind in the shelter of the woods. The snow delighted Tracy and Nan.

"I think I remember snow from way back when I was a child," Tracy said, "but we never had any in California."

"I don't remember it at all," Nan admitted. "Is it good to eat?"

"There's no taste to it, but it won't hurt you," Sally assured her. They all sampled the snow and agreed that it was merely cold.

"Too bad your little brother couldn't come," Sally ventured. This was prying, but she had learned long ago that sometimes you had to pry to get information. Right now she wanted to learn more about Benjie. "Rhoda and Ben are some old disappointed not to see him."

"Benjie? He's nothing to see," Tracy informed her. "He just sits wherever you put him, like a—I don't know what. A block of wood."

"Tracy!" Sally was shocked. "He's your baby brother! I wish I had a brother."

"You wouldn't want a brother like Benjie," Nan said. "All the other kids at school ask questions about him and laugh."

"We don't invite the others home to play with us anymore," Tracy announced. "They talk behind our backs about Benjie, and make fun—" She sounded as though she were going to cry.

"People can be pretty stinking mean sometimes," Sally offered in comfort. "You don't want to pay any attention to them."

"That's what Mother says. Or she used to say it. Now she and Daddy have decided that it's best for all of us —for Benjie, too—if he doesn't live with us anymore." Tracy kicked a snow-covered bush. "Her friends are just as stinking mean about Benjie as ours are. She says that now we've moved to a new place and are making new friends—" She left the sentence unfinished.

So that was the trouble, Sally thought. They were all ashamed of Benjie and didn't want him around. Poor little boy. Poor Nan and Tracy and Laurel and Nathan, too, she supposed. You certainly couldn't tell by looking at a family whether they were happy or not. Everybody had their problems, she guessed.

"Oooh, Tracy, what you said!" Nan was pleasurably horrified. "Stinking! You'd better not let Mother hear you—"

Sally was glad of the change of subject. "And you'd better not tell Ben and Rhoda I said it first. They'd skin me alive."

"Why do you call them Ben and Rhoda? They're grown-up. It's disrespectful." Nan was plainly proud of that word.

"Well, I don't have any family of my own, so I live around with different people and I call them whatever they want me to. Sometimes I call them Uncle and Aunt, and sometimes I call them Mister and Missus, and sometimes—"

Sally rattled on, answering questions about other homes in which she had been placed, making her life as a State Kid sound interesting and exciting. She surprised even herself with the glowing picture she painted. To hear me talk, she thought wryly, anybody would think I chose to be a State Kid.

But her imaginary adventures served to divert Tracy and Nan, and by the time they arrived back at the house, Benjie had been forgotten.

CHAPTER 3

Apparently Benjie had been forgotten at the house, too. Whatever was to be said on the subject of Benjie had evidently been said. At least, his name was not mentioned during the meal that Rhoda had been planning all week long.

"We'll have a real Down-East dinner," she had said. "Clam chowder and lobster with all the fixings, topped off with blueberry pie and maybe Indian pudding as well. They'll relish that, them having been in foreign parts so long." To Rhoda, California was about as foreign as a part could be.

Everybody seemed to enjoy the meal as much as Rhoda had predicted. If there had been a disagreement between the older and the younger Coopers, they had decided to put it aside, or perhaps Nathan and Laurel had convinced Ben and Rhoda that their decision was the right one. In either case, talk flowed smoothly and pleasantly, with good-natured laughter over Tracy and Nan's efforts to cope with their lobsters. Sally could remember her first one, back in her early days on the island. She had wondered then how the first lobster-eater had had the courage to tackle the ugly things. But she had learned the trick of extracting the tender meat from the hard red shells. There was nothing to it, once you caught on, she assured Tracy; and it was certainly worth a little trouble.

Rhoda would not let the guests help with the dish-washing. "No. Sally and I'll make short shrift of them after you've gone. We see you so seldom, I don't want to waste any of your visit doing dishes. I do wish you'd change your minds and stay overnight."

"I wish we could," Laurel told her politely, "but it's a long drive back to Boston. I want Nathan to get a good rest tomorrow. Monday is his first day on the new job and he'll have to be on his toes. In fact"—she looked at her watch and at the declining sun—"much as I hate to break up this party, I do think we should be starting. It gets dark so early this time of the year."

Everybody started bustling around, finding coats and misplaced mittens. Almost before she knew it, Sally found herself standing on the wharf with Rhoda, waving after the departing boat. Laurel, she thought, was a great little old organizer, for all her polite manner. Rhoda was probably right when she said that Nathan owed his rapid promotion to Laurel. Well, you certainly couldn't blame a woman for helping her husband get ahead in the world. Probably the whole idea of sending

Benjie away to school had been Laurel's. Benjie simply wouldn't fit into Laurel's idea of a rising young businessman's family.

As though she had read Sally's mind, Rhoda said, "I just don't see how she can do it. Send Benjie away, I mean. Why, she's his *mother*."

Sally felt an old familiar pang. "My mother did it to me," she muttered.

"Oh, Sally, I'm sorry." Rhoda was honestly distressed. "I didn't think. Listen, you've got to believe that your mother couldn't help herself. We don't know the circumstances—"

"It's all right, Rhoda. Don't worry. I've got used to the

idea. Like Miss Bridges says, I'm adjusted." "Adjust" was a favorite word of social workers, she had found. It meant making the best of a bad deal.

"With Nathan and Laurel, it's different. There's no earthly reason why they can't keep Benjie at home where he belongs. I don't know about Laurel, but Nathan wasn't brought up this way. I'm so mad at him I could snatch him bald-headed." Rhoda was stamping up the road in a fury. "He was brought up to believe that families stuck together and took care of their own. When I think of our first grandson being shoved away out of sight like that, I could spit nails. What if he is a little slow?" She was talking to herself as much as to Sally. "Island families have had slow children before this. A couple of them have been downright feeble-minded. We used to call them 'innocents.' Nobody dreamed of sending them off someplace. They stayed right here in the village, and everybody kept an eye on them to see that they came to no harm, and nobody thought the less of their families for their misfortune. I'd like to get my hands on Benjie and bring him out here where I could—"

She stopped in the middle of the road so abruptly that Sally, a step behind, ran into her. Rhoda did not notice. "My land," she said in a tone almost of awe, "now why didn't I think of that before? That Laurel! She's such a plausible talker, she addled my wits, I guess. Ben ought to have thought of it. Benjie's his namesake, after all." She looked around at Sally and laughed. "Listen to me,

❦ 29

putting the blame on everyone else when the truth is that I'm the one who's been plain stupid."

"Maybe they won't let him come," Sally ventured.

Rhoda began walking again, less angrily now. "Oh, they'll let him come, all right. Ben and I'll see to that, if we have to kidnap him"—she turned into her own dooryard and climbed the kitchen steps—"though I don't suppose for a minute it'll come to that. Laurel talked a lot about 'the best thing for the child' "—her voice was an exact mimicry of Laurel's—"but I got the impression that it was six of one and half a dozen of the other. She was thinking of herself, too. She won't care much where he is, so long as he's in good hands and out of sight."

"Maybe you're right," Sally said. "I got that impression, too, from some things Tracy and Nan said. You know, about the kids at school giving them a hard time about their brother. I know how that is. It isn't easy. This is the first school I ever went to that they didn't give me a hard time about being a State Kid."

Rhoda glanced at her sympathetically and handed her a dish towel. "There's two sides to every story, of course. I hadn't ought to think too harshly of Laurel and Nathan. I never lived on the main, and I don't know how things are over there. I ought not to sit in judgment. They're probably doing the right thing as they see it." She brightened as she poured boiling water over the clean dishes. "I'm not going to fret about that. All I'm going to worry about is how soon Benjie can get here."

🌱 30

There was never any question about Benjie's coming to live with his grandparents, once Rhoda suggested it to Ben. Since there was no telephone on the island, the Coopers made the trip to Stillport the next day, to call up Nathan and Laurel. They came back looking pleased.

"We talked to both of them," Rhoda reported to Sally. "Laurel sounded a little doubtful at first. Said she didn't know if the school would approve. *Approve*, mind you!" Her voice dripped scorn. "But I guess Nathan put his foot down, for once. I knew in my bones that he was enough of an island boy so that the whole idea went against his grain. I'm glad he had the gumption to stand up for what he believes. Anyhow, it's all arranged. Nathan'll be bringing Benjie down next weekend." She almost sang the words.

"That's nice." In spite of her very real relief that Benjie was not going to be rejected as she herself had been, Sally's tone was subdued.

Ben looked at her sharply. Ben never said much, but that didn't mean that he didn't do a lot of thinking. Sometimes Sally was startled by the keenness of his observation. This was one of the times.

"If you're wondering," he said slowly, "whether this will make a difference as far as you're concerned, you can just quit worrying. It won't make a mite of difference. That I promise you."

Sally flushed. Ben had hit on the truth. She had lived with families who had small children of their own. No matter how hard they tried to be fair and impartial, they always favored their own flesh and blood. Probably they themselves didn't always realize it, because the signs were often so small: just a different tone of voice, a fond gesture, a little loving glance. But these little things were enough to mark all over again the line between the outsider and the one who belonged. She had been alone here with Ben and Rhoda. They had made her feel like the queen bee. She couldn't help wondering how much things would change with Benjie's coming.

"Why, Ben! The very idea!" Rhoda was indignant. "Of course it won't make any difference in how we feel about Sally. You're like a daughter to me, Sally—sometimes almost like a younger sister, you've got such an old head on your shoulders. I take real comfort from you. Nothing's going to change that." She meant it.

Sally felt like hugging her. "I'll help you all I can," she promised eagerly. "Benjie will make more work—"

"Now don't try to teach your grandmother to suck eggs," Rhoda admonished, using an old island expression. "I've raised three boys already, remember." Her face sobered. "Benjie's different, I realize. Laurel warned me that he'd need a lot more time and care than most, him being like he is. But my land, I've got all the time in the world, and with you to lend a hand—"

She'd lend both hands, Sally determined. She'd do anything in the world for Rhoda and Ben.

CHAPTER 4

No matter what you told people, or how carefully you explained things to them, Sally thought, they didn't really believe you until they saw for themselves. She had no idea what Rhoda had expected in Benjie, but it was clearly not this.

Nathan had come into the kitchen, leading Benjie, and for a moment they had been the ideal picture of handsome father and small, handsome son. Benjie was a beautiful child, beautifully dressed and cared for, with Nathan and Rhoda's dark hair and eyes. Rhoda stepped forward with outstretched arms, laughing softly and saying happily, "There's his grandma's darling boy! Has he got a big kiss for Grandma?"

Sally watched Rhoda's smile fade, heard her voice falter as she repeated, "A kiss for Grandma?", saw the shock overspread her face.

For Benjie showed no response at all—no interest, no friendliness, not even the shyness that would have been natural. His eyes were as blank and empty as the windows of a deserted house. That was what he was like,

Sally thought—an abandoned house. Nobody lived in the well-formed four-year-old body.

A sudden recollection came to her. She had seen a child like this before, years ago, in one of the shelters. He could walk, if someone led him. He whimpered, if hurt or cold or hungry. He ate if someone fed him, and drank from a cup held to his lips. But left alone, he sat quietly for hours, like a life-sized doll. They said he could see and hear perfectly well, and that he would be as bright and active as anybody, if— If what? Nobody knew.

Sally wondered fleetingly and with pity whatever became of that other little boy who had no grandparents to take him in.

Now, however, she could feel concern only for Rhoda, who looked so stricken. She wanted to throw her arms around her, to tell her that everything would work out fine. But nothing in her life had encouraged her to give easy gestures of affection, and who knew how things were going to work out? Perhaps the kindest thing she could do for Rhoda right now would be simply to leave her alone with her family, to give them all time by themselves to—well, yes, adjust. She wrinkled her nose at the use of the word, shrugged into her heavy jacket, and quietly let herself out the kitchen door. She'd go over to Linda's for a while.

Linda was busy making a bird feeder out of an empty plastic bleach-water jug. Miss Mills, the teacher, was a wildlife enthusiast, and she had suggested that feeding the birds during the winter months would be not only humane and educational, but interesting as well.

"It is, too," Linda told Sally. "Ma made me a couple of bait bags yesterday, and I filled them with suet and hung them in that apple tree out back." Bait bags were the twine mesh sacks that the lobstermen filled with decayed fish to bait their lobster traps. "I've already got chickadees and two kinds of sparrows coming to them."

"Birds," Sally said disgustedly. "Big deal."

Linda ignored that and held up the jug, in the sides of which she had cut two large holes. "There. Now all I've got to do is put a handle on it to hang it up by, and fill it with birdseed. Pa got me some yesterday, over on the main. Hand me that piece of wire, Sally."

When the feeder was done, Sally rather reluctantly went out with Linda to hang it in the tree. She had more important things on her mind than a bunch of silly birds, and she had expected her best friend to show a little interest in her problems. She sighed deeply a few times, hoping that Linda would ask sympathetic questions, but Linda was absorbed in her project. That was like Linda, Sally thought. She had a one-track mind, and right now it was tracking birds.

"Nathan brought his little boy over to live with us today," Sally said finally. She had learned that all the islanders, living as they did so far out of the world, were intensely interested in any little item of news. This one ought to get Linda's attention.

But all Linda said was, "Did he? That's good. Hey,

look!" She pointed at a chickadee, pert and saucy in its black cap and bib. "Isn't he the bold thing? I'll bet I can get them to eating out of my hand in no time at all."

Several more chickadees swirled in like an eddy of blown leaves, perching on twigs and eyeing the girls fearlessly and curiously. In spite of herself, Sally had to admit that they were cute little things. Maybe she should make a bird feeder of her own. Rhoda would help her. Rhoda was always interested in doing new things.

Or always had been. Now that Benjie was here, she wouldn't have as much time for Sally. Sally had better be thinking about helping Rhoda, not the other way round.

"I've got to go home and help Rhoda," she said.

But Linda was watching her chickadees. "See you tomorrow," she answered absently.

Ben and Nathan had left for the mainland when Sally entered the house. Rhoda was sitting in the rocking chair by the window overlooking the harbor, with Benjie in her lap. She was stroking his dark hair gently; but her eyes, fixed on something far away, were almost as expressionless as his.

Sally's heart went out to her. She looked so sad. Rhoda was never sad. Serious, sometimes—and cross once in a while—but never sad. Sally hung her jacket on a peg near the door and said cheerily, "Hi. I came home to help you." She advanced across the floor and unconsciously raised her voice. "Hi there, Benjie."

"Shh! He's not deaf," Rhoda told her sharply. Then

37

she seemed to sag. "I'm sorry, Sally. I didn't mean to snap at you. But one of the things Nathan warned us about was shouting at Benjie. It's natural, when somebody doesn't seem to hear, but it doesn't do any good and it might do harm. Nobody likes to be hollered at, not even—" Her voice trailed off.

Sally changed the subject. "Don't you want me to put Benjie's things away or something?"

Rhoda brightened. "That would be nice. His clothes go in— But you know as well as I do. You helped me fix up his room for him."

When Sally came down from attending to Benjie's belongings, Rhoda was still sitting by the window, holding Benjie.

"Boy!" Sally exclaimed. "Wait till you see his clothes. They're good enough for a little prince."

"Oh, Laurel keeps him nice, that I'll admit," Rhoda said a little grudgingly. "You couldn't want for a better-tended young one. It's her giving him up that I hold against her. Though maybe—"

"Maybe it's for the best," Sally finished the sentence for her, and promptly decided that it was a meaningless remark. "Here, let me hold him for a while, while you—"

"No. He's my responsibility, and I don't intend to shirk it."

That was Rhoda. She carried her own loads.

"Then I'll start supper, if you'll tell me what you're going to have. Ben'll be back pretty soon."

"No, that's my job. When you came here, there was a

clear understanding with Miss Bridges about what I·could ask of you—"

"You're not asking," Sally pointed out. "I'm offering because I want to, and that's not the same."

Rhoda wavered. "Well, maybe then, just this once, to give Benjie a chance to get used to me. It's important, Nathan said, that he gets used to his surroundings. He has to feel *secure*—that's the word that Nathan used. All this shifting around from California to Boston to that school, then here—"

"That's enough to make the Rock of Gibraltar feel insecure," Sally said. "I'd ought to know."

As she started supper preparations she thought of the years during which she herself had been shifted from foster home to foster home, and how lost she had felt. She guessed she'd been lucky, though. Somewhere along the line it had occurred to her that she was Sally Gray, no matter where she lived. That was one thing she could depend on, the one thing nobody could take away from her.

After that, things hadn't been so bad. Her last foster mother had told her that she was too independent. So all right—she was too independent. That was better than just giving herself up and becoming like a piece of dough that anybody could poke into any shape, perhaps even into a shape like Benjie's.

CHAPTER 5

Ben had said that everything would be the same as far as Sally was concerned, after Benjie came; but things were not the same. Ben himself was no different. Of course, Sally did not see a great deal of him. She never had. He was usually out of the house before either the sun or Sally was up in the morning. When he came in from hauling his lobster traps, she was in school. Afternoons he spent down by the harborside in his shop, a gray-shingled building perched on long stilts above the water, where he built traps, painted lobster buoys, and mended gear.

When he was at home he was his old self, interested in Sally's news of school and the other children, occasionally joking with her a little. When he went to Stillport he still brought her back a candy bar or a couple of oranges. Ben was the same as always.

It was Rhoda who had changed. She kept her house as spotless as ever, and served her customary good meals promptly. On washdays she hung out even bigger washings than before to bleach and dry in the stiff salt breeze and pale winter sunshine. But she never went to the store as she used to do, lingering to gossip and laugh with the other women. Sally and Ben did her errands for her. On fine days she walked in the yard with Benjie, holding his hand tightly as he moved beside her like a mechanical toy. But she never crossed the road to chat with Rose Allen, Linda's mother. One day after school, when Sally offered to sit with Benjie so that Rhoda could run up to the Chandlers' or down to the Coles' to visit with her friends Emma and Minerva, Rhoda refused.

"Thank you, Sally, but I guess I won't. I'd be nervous as a cat all the time I was gone, wondering if Benjie was all right."

"He'd be all right. I'd be right here. I wouldn't take my eyes off him for a second." Sally crossed her heart solemnly. "Not for one second, I swear."

"I know. But I wouldn't draw an easy breath. His coming here was my idea, and if anything happened to him, I don't know how I could face Nathan and Laurel. Besides, he has to get used to me. That's important. They said so at the school."

Oh, blast the school! Sally thought rebelliously. Rhoda ought to use a little sense about what they said. She ought to get out once in a while, instead of staying cooped up here in the house like a prisoner. Benjie wouldn't notice. He didn't notice anything. He hadn't improved a bit in the three weeks he'd been on the island. He just sat there. He was a pain in the neck.

"I didn't mean that!" Sally told herself quickly,

shocked. "Poor Benjie, it isn't his fault. I'm sorry for him, really. It's only that—"

It was only that Rhoda had no time for her anymore. Rhoda used to be fun, and now she wasn't. She and Sally used to do things together, and now they didn't.

"I don't suppose you feel like helping me make a bird feeder?" Sally asked experimentally. She really didn't care much about making one, but she wanted terribly to share something with Rhoda again, and a bird feeder was the first thing that came into her mind. "Miss Mills wants us to keep lists of the birds we see. She's going to give a prize for the best list." All this was true, although up until now Sally had considered the whole thing a bore. "All I need is a plastic jug and a piece of wire. I can borrow some birdseed from Linda."

To her surprise, Rhoda seized on the idea. Maybe she missed the old comradeship as much as Sally did. "I've got a jug that's almost empty. I can pour the bleach into something else. There must be some old ends of wire out in the shed. Find that good sharp paring knife—"

Rhoda was tackling the project with something of her old spirit. She gave only an occasional glance at Benjie, silent and unaware in his chair by the window. She and Sally were just finishing their task at dusk, when Ben came up from the harbor.

He entered quietly, and then stopped short. "Well!" he exclaimed. "I see you've been bit by the bug. Every dooryard on the island has got one of them things dan-

gling in it, and I been wondering when the fever would catch up with you two."

This was a longer speech than Sally had heard Ben make in weeks—since Benjie came, it occurred to her. She realized suddenly that the change in Rhoda had been hard on Ben, too, although—being Ben—he had never complained.

"If you can't lick 'em, join 'em, like the feller says," Sally told him flippantly, and was pleased to hear him chuckle. "I'll go over to Linda's and borrow some birdseed, and then we can hang the feeder in that lilac bush right outside the window. That way, we can watch the birds without going outside and freezing to death."

"Tomorrow's Friday, mail day," Ben observed. "I'll get hold of Hiram Grant on the ferry, over the shortwave, and tell him to bring over a couple of bags of seed. We might as well do this thing up proper."

"My land, is tomorrow Friday already? I sort of lose track of the days, staying so close to home." Rhoda looked at the calendar on the wall. "First Friday in February. That means the social worker'll be coming over from the main to check up on how bad we're abusing you, Sally." It wasn't much of a joke, but it was nice to have Rhoda joke at all. She had been pretty sobersided for the past three weeks.

The two social workers, Miss Carr and Miss Bridges, alternated the monthly visits to the island required by their jobs with the Child Welfare Department. This month, Sally was glad to remember, it was Miss Bridges' turn. Miss Carr was all right, but Miss Bridges had had charge of Sally's case as far back as Sally could recall. She was the one person in the world whom Sally had known all her life. She had known plenty of people— too many, really—but all the others had vanished after longer or shorter periods. Miss Bridges was still around, getting a little grayer each year, but still tough and dependable. Sally considered her a friend, or as much a friend as you could ever get to be with a caseworker.

She was really happy to find Miss Bridges sitting in the kitchen with Rhoda, over cups of tea, when she came home from school the next day.

"It's easy to see that you're flourishing, Sally," Miss Bridges greeted her. "It's actually a waste of time for me to come out here to Star Island. I know before I start that I'm not going to run into any serious problems." She put down her teacup and stood up, looking around for her coat. "There's no need of my lingering. Mr. Cole is taking me back to Stillport, and he'll want to be starting soon." The ferry returned to the mainland before the social workers could complete their visits, so one of the lobstermen always returned them instead. "Want to walk me down to the harbor, Sally?"

All three of them knew that this was a tactful way of arranging for the private talk that Miss Bridges was obliged to have with Sally, but they all pretended otherwise.

"Sure," Sally said. "Want anything at the store, Rhoda?"

❧ 45

"The birdseed, if it came. And you might pick up some milk and some soda crackers." Rhoda saw them to the door and stood watching as they walked down the path.

Miss Bridges came directly to the point. "Your situation has changed a little since my last visit. How do you like having the Coopers' little grandson here?"

"Benjie?" Sally shrugged. "He's their grandson, like you said. He's got more right here than I have. I guess I have to like it."

"Whether you like it or not? Come on, Sally. You're usually outspoken enough. What's the trouble?"

Sally shrugged again. "Nothing, I guess. Things aren't like they used to be, that's all. Rhoda's all wrapped up in Benjie. She never has time to do the things we used to do, like going over to the back shore to look for seashells, or—well, anything."

"And you're feeling neglected. Tell me this. Are you really neglected? Are you getting proper meals and proper care? You know what the Welfare Department standards are as well as I do. Are they being met?"

"Of course they are!" Sally was indignant. "What do you think Rhoda is? She wouldn't neglect a stray dog." She thought a moment. "I guess I'm a little jealous of Benjie and all the attention she gives him." It was a new idea to her, but she realized that it was true.

"That's one of the things I like about you," Miss Bridges said. "You're honest with yourself, even if it hurts. Frankly, I'm not sure that all this attention Mrs. Cooper gives Benjie is the best thing for him. I saw how it is while I was there just now. It seemed to me that she was being overprotective—almost smothering, you might say. I'm not a child psychiatrist, but in my work you're bound to pick up a smattering of knowledge. I've seen a few cases like Benjie."

Sally stopped short in the middle of the road. "Then you can talk to Rhoda, tell her—Let's go right back now."

"Oh, Sally, Sally! You know I can't do that. Benjie's not a ward of the state, and I have no authority whatsoever to interfere. Furthermore, I'm not a specialist in the field of mental health, and I could easily give wrong advice."

"I suppose so." Sally started walking again. "You say you've seen cases like Benjie. Do they ever get better?"

"Yes, sometimes, though it's something you can't predict. It seems to be a question of getting through the shell that surrounds a child like that. Once that's accomplished, the children usually make up for lost time very fast. One little girl that I happen to know about never said one word until she was five years old. Then one day, for no reason that anybody could see, she began talking in complete sentences, using a surprisingly good vocabulary. She graduated from high school last year, the second in her class."

"Then you think maybe Benjie—?"

"Sally, how can I tell? I know of other cases that never got better. It would be nice if there were some sure cure, but there isn't. Until we know more about the mind and how it works, all we can do is try. Patience and love seem to be the best remedies, until we find something better. In the meantime"—Miss Bridges smiled and put a hand on Sally's arm—"try not to resent Benjie. He needs—"

"Ready to go, Miss Bridges?" a man's voice broke in, and Lon Cole swung into step with them. "I'll put you across in no time flat."

Miss Bridges said good-bye and went off with Lon, and Sally turned in at the store to do Rhoda's errands. Walking up the hill with her parcels, she thought about what Miss Bridges had said. She, Sally, had been resenting Benjie, and she knew it now. She ought to be ashamed of herself, and she was. But knowing and being ashamed were not enough. She would have to do better than that.

The westering sun was low over the mainland as she approached home, and the lilac bush where the bird feeder hung was lively with birds. Late afternoon and early morning were the times of day when they seemed hungriest.

She stopped for a moment to watch them, pleased that they appreciated her efforts in their behalf. There were the little chickadees darting through the branches, and two noisy blue jays, and some large yellow birds with black and white wings that must be grosbeaks. She had heard about grosbeaks at school, during bird study, the new class that Miss Mills had recently introduced. If she didn't watch out, Sally told herself, she'd be as nutty about birds as the rest of the kids. Already she was beginning to enjoy watching the birds, and that was a bad sign.

Then she realized that she was not the only watcher. Through the slender branches of the bush she could see the kitchen window, framing Benjie's head and shoulders. He was sitting as always in his chair, staring out at nothing. If you could call that watching. Sally shook her head. You would think that all those birds fluttering and screeching and fighting practically smack in his face and eyes would make him at least blink a little. If they didn't snap him out of whatever ailed him, she guessed that nothing would. Poor Rhoda.

With the idea of cheering Rhoda up, Sally leaped up the steps and flung the door open with a whoop. "Hey, Rhoda, did you see all the birds we've got?"

"Sally, *please!*" Rhoda's voice was carefully controlled, but she was angry. "I've told you over and over about hollering. You know what the school said." She moved over to stand protectively beside Benjie.

"Sorry," Sally muttered. "Here are your things from the store." She plunked them down on the table. She'd be darned if she'd knock herself out again trying to cheer up Rhoda. Let her work out her own problems. "Is it okay if I go over to Linda's for a while?" She did not wait for an answer, but slammed out of the house.

She was halfway across the road before she remembered that only a very short time ago she had promised herself not to be resentful of Benjie and his hold on Rhoda. Keeping that promise was not going to be as easy as making it had been.

CHAPTER 6

Miss Mills came back from the February vacation and announced that thereafter the older pupils would be given homework to do. Although the Starhaven school was so small that each student had a great deal of individual attention and there was plenty of time for seatwork while Miss Mills was hearing other grades recite, she thought homework would be good preparation for the high school years to come. Besides, she said, this would give the pupils extra time in school for more advanced subjects than those required. Miss Mills took her job seriously. She was not satisfied with merely meeting the state requirements. She fully intended to surpass them.

"If you've got any errands for me to do," Sally told Rhoda after school, "I'd better do them now. Once I get started on my homework, I don't want to be interrupted." Having homework to do made her feel important, almost like a college student.

Rhoda looked at her with a glint in her eye, not quite smiling, and Sally felt a little foolish. "Oh, it's not that big a deal," she admitted. "All we've got to do is write a composition about anything we want to. Usually Miss Mills assigns a topic, but this time she's letting us choose. She says to give our imaginations free rein."

"It's hard to decide," Rhoda remembered from her own long-ago school days. "There's so many things— What have you chosen?"

"Oh, I don't know. Maybe something about this mad scientist, and he was experimenting with a secret formula—Or how about a girl that got lost in the African jungle? She could be in the Peace Corps—"

Rhoda laughed. "Or how about something nearer home? It usually helps to know what you're talking about, I'm told."

"I suppose so, only there's nothing very exciting— Hey, I could have a fugitive from justice sneak onto Star Island and hide in the woods, and he could keep stealing things at night—food and stuff—and we all blame each other, and an awful feud starts—"

"That's giving your imagination free rein, all right," Rhoda commented dryly. "I hope you'll arrange to have him caught before we all kill each other off."

Sally nodded absently, her mind already busy with the capture, for which a girl with a large mouth and red hair would be chiefly responsible, after older and wiser heads had failed to solve the Mystery of Star Island. She cleared a space on the kitchen table, found paper and a pencil, and sat down to work, already absorbed in her composition.

When Rhoda said, "I'm going out now and get the clothes off the line," Sally only nodded. She was too busy thinking, to answer. She'd have another girl, she decided, a rich summer girl off a yacht. She had everything —money, beauty, a big-shot family—but she didn't know beans about anything that mattered. This escaped convict would capture her and hold her for ransom, and—

She started scribbling furiously, but after a few moments the flow of her thoughts faltered. She felt strangely uncomfortable. In one school she had attended over on the main, they used to play a game of staring hard at someone's back, trying to make him turn around. That was just the way she felt now. But that was ridiculous. Rhoda was out in the clothesyard, and there was no one here except Benjie. He certainly didn't count. Being alone with Benjie was like being alone, period. There was just about as much life behind his gaze as behind that of a graven image. Unless Rhoda was staring in the window—

Sally got up and looked out into the yard. Rhoda was there all right, tugging the sheets off the line and whacking their frozen folds into submission.

Sally shrugged. The feeling was gone now. It had probably been her imagination. She went back to her composition. It wouldn't be very smart of the convict to call attention to himself by snatching the rich girl. Maybe she'd throw the rich girl out altogether. Who needed her? Instead, she'd have the redheaded girl, whose name was Penelope, happen to look out the window one night and see by the light of the moon—

Again Sally felt creepy, as though someone were spying on her. Maybe a stray cat had somehow slipped into the house and was peering at her from under the stove or somewhere. Feeling foolish, she got up and looked behind and under every piece of furniture. There was nobody in the room except Benjie, and that meant nobody. She was simply being silly, scaring herself with her own escaped convict.

Then Rhoda came in with her heaping basket of laundry, bringing a breath of cold air and the wonderful fresh smell of clean clothes just off the line. Sally forgot her uneasiness in Rhoda's brisk presence.

A few days later, on a cold and drizzly afternoon, Matt Cole knocked at the kitchen door. Larry Scott and the Chandlers' black dog, Mate, were with him. His mother had sent him, he told Rhoda, to get Rhoda's recipe for Anadama bread, handed down to her from her great-great-grandmother.

"I'll find it and copy it off for you," Rhoda said. "Come in, boys, and shut the door. No sense in wasting good firewood heating all outdoors. Leave the dog outside. A little cold and wet won't hurt him."

Mate had other ideas. The boys had been in school all day, and he had missed them. Where they went, he intended to go. He pushed his way into the kitchen, wagging his tail, sure of his welcome.

"Oh, all right," Rhoda conceded. "Just so long as he

behaves himself. One peep out of him to upset Benjie, and out he goes."

"Don't worry. We'll be quiet," Matt assured her. By this time, everyone on Star Island knew that Rhoda would tolerate no noise or disturbance near Benjie. "Okay if we look at Ben's new catalog?"

Rhoda said it was all right, took from a drawer the scrapbook in which she pasted special recipes, and sat down to copy the one Minerva Cole wanted. Sally addressed a few remarks to Matt and Larry, but they were too absorbed in the catalog of marine supplies to answer her. She tried to get Mate to shake hands with her, but the kitchen was new territory to him. He could not be bothered with tricks when there were so many strange odors and odd corners to investigate.

Sally gave up and leaned against the sink resignedly. She might just as well be in a roomful of Benjies, she thought, with everybody so wrapped up in themselves they couldn't even see or hear her. Not that she cared, really. She had simply been trying to be sociable. But if nobody wanted to talk, she would keep her big mouth shut, too. Her glance wandered over the others—over Rhoda, busy with her copying, over the boys, absorbed in the price of potwarp, over Mate, nosing around Benjie's chair, over Benjie—

She stiffened. There was something odd about Benjie —something different. Then she relaxed. She could have sworn that Benjie was really looking at Mate, that there

had been a gleam of interest in his eyes as the great
rough head brushed close past his knees. But of course
she was mistaken. It must have been the way the light
shone through the window on Benjie's face that had
fooled her. Now that she looked hard, he was the same
as always—blank, empty-eyed, shut away.

In the days that followed, however, Sally could not
rid herself of the notion that something had come and
gone in Benjie's eyes on that raw and rainy afternoon
when Mate had come calling. Had whoever lived in the
empty house opened the door a crack and then slammed
it shut before she could be sure? The whole thing had
been so fleeting, like the glint of a sunbeam on a hum-

mingbird's wing. There was nothing you could pin down in your own mind so that you could say positively, "This happened." She didn't know whether it happened or not. The only way to be certain was to wait and watch. Two could play at that game; she and the one in hiding—if there was anyone hiding.

So she watched. Sometimes she kept her eyes fixed on Benjie's face so long and steadily that they watered. Nothing happened. Once she had the feeling, when she closed her eyes to rest them, that someone was watching her in turn. It was the same feeling she'd had on the day when she had written her composition. Did Benjie, when it was safe, notice people? She didn't know. When she turned, he was as lifeless as always. Yet she had the maddening feeling that if she had been a little quicker— It was like glimpsing something moving just outside the field of vision, and turning too late to catch it.

She wondered if Rhoda ever had the same feeling when she was alone with Benjie. Surely she would have mentioned it. But perhaps not. Perhaps, like Sally, she was shy of trying to put into words anything so vague, anything that might after all be only imagination.

There was one way of finding out. "Rhoda," Sally said hesitantly one afternoon, "have you noticed any change in Benjie lately? Like something's stirring around inside him, kind of?"

Rhoda made an impatient sound. "Oh, stop, Sally. Of course not. And don't go around putting ideas in my head. Seems like I've got enough to contend with already." She sounded driven and cross. "If there was any change in Benjie, I'd be the first to see it, being with him as much as I am. Give up your crazy notions and leave Benjie to me. Here, if you want to be useful, take this plate back to Minerva's."

So that was that. Rhoda had noticed nothing different about Benjie. Sally had been fooling herself, inventing things to pass the short, drab days of winter. From now on, she would leave Benjie to Rhoda, tend her own pea patch, and forget the whole thing. She took the plate—now piled with filled cookies—on which Minerva had sent a sample of the Anadama bread, and let herself out of the house.

She did not hurry back. She whiled away some time playing with the Coles' cat, dropped in at Linda's to see what she was doing, and stayed to talk with her and her mother. It was almost sunset by the time she crossed the road and entered her own yard. As always at this time of day, the birds were busy around the feeder, and she stopped for a moment to inspect them. She had given up pretending to a lack of interest in them. They really were sort of fascinating, and she might as well admit it.

As a tiny, fierce song sparrow chased a grosbeak four times its size away from some seeds that had spilled on the ground she grinned delightedly, and looked up at the kitchen window to see if Rhoda had observed the fight. Rhoda was nowhere in sight. Only Benjie's head and shoulders were visible through the glass. The birds meant nothing to him. He just sat there, looking out at

nothing, even if he did give the impression of attention. Anybody who didn't know better would think, just by looking at him, that—

Sally froze. The level rays of the setting sun shone full on Benjie's face, and she could see it clearly. He was —he really was!—noticing the birds. She couldn't possibly be wrong. His eyes were moving from side to side with the darting of the chickadees to and from the suet bag, and they followed the bright flash of a blue jay as it flew from the ground to the highest branch of the lilac. She had not been mistaken during these past days. Shyly, stealthily, Benjie was peering out of his prison.

Moving slowly, Sally opened the door and entered the

kitchen. She did not want to distract or frighten Benjie. She wanted Rhoda to see what she had seen.

"Rhoda," she said very quietly.

Rhoda jumped, gave a little scream, and dropped an empty saucepan that she had been holding.

"Good grief, Sally, you almost scared the living daylights out of me, creeping up on me like that!" she exclaimed. "Give a body a little warning that you're around, for mercy's sake!"

Sally's heart sank as she looked at Benjie. There was no spark of life in his face. His eyes were as blank as marbles. The scream, the clatter of the pan, Rhoda's sharp tone, had driven the fugitive back into hiding.

"I'm sorry, Rhoda," she said. "I didn't mean to startle you."

There was no use in telling Rhoda what she had seen. Rhoda would not believe her. She had already accused her once this afternoon of having crazy notions about Benjie. To believe, Rhoda would have to see for herself.

CHAPTER 7

In what Sally had come to think of as "the olden days," the days before Benjie's arrival, she had spent long hours with Rhoda. Often Linda had come over, and the three of them had made popcorn balls or played pounce. This was a simple card game involving much slapping down of cards and a great deal of shouting and laughing. It had been fun.

Now Linda seldom came in, and when she did, it was only for a moment. It was no fun just hanging around the house being quiet. As Linda said, life was too short.

So Sally kept her room neat, helped with the dishes, did Rhoda's errands, and occasionally swept and dusted. When these tasks were completed, she went elsewhere. There was plenty to do on the island and no danger of getting into real trouble. You couldn't get lost or run over or kidnapped. The worst thing that could happen to you would be to fall in the ocean, and even then you'd probably only get wet.

It would be different, Sally told herself, if staying home did anybody any good. But it didn't. Rhoda wouldn't let her help with Benjie. She often seemed impatient when Sally tried to cheer her up with reports of school or bits of gossip she'd heard at the store. So, on stormy days, Sally went over to Linda's. In fine weather she accompanied Miss Mills and the other children on what Miss Mills called nature walks; or she joined the others in coasting on tin trays down the steep, icy slope above the village; or she took part in a snowball fight in the school yard. She had to admit that she enjoyed herself thoroughly.

One Saturday, however, she found herself at loose ends after she had finished her chores. Linda had gone over to the mainland with her family for the day. The six smaller schoolchildren were in the Wells's yard, building a snowman. Sally went over and started to help them, but she soon saw that they did not want her help. When Billy Wells told her that she was too bossy and to get out of his yard or he'd tell his mother, she washed her hands of that affair and wandered out into the road.

Larry Scott, Tom Smith, and Matt Cole were coming up the hill, and Sally waited for them. Matt was an island boy, while Tom and Larry were State Kids like herself. All three were about her own age.

"Hi, fellers," she greeted them. "What's up?"

"We're going over on the Backside," Tom told her. The Backside was the outer shore of the island—a wild stretch of coast constantly exposed to storms and high seas. "With this sea running, we'd ought to find some good gear washed up."

Sally had to smile. The way Tom talked now, you'd think he'd been born on the island, and his grandfather and great-grandfather before him. She could remember —and it wasn't so very long ago—when he hadn't known a lobster trap from kiss-my-elbow. She cocked her head and listened. Now that Tom mentioned it, she could hear the low, dull roar of the surf, more like a vibration in the air than an actual sound.

"Guess I'll go with you," she said. At least it was something to do.

"And I guess you won't," Matt informed her. " 'Tain't no place for a girl."

Sometimes Matt made her good and mad. Usually he was an all-right guy, but once in a while he got on his high horse and acted as if he were the king of the island.

"I'd like to see you stop me," she retorted. "You and two more like you." She gave Tom and Larry her meanest look. "It's a free country, and I'm as able to take care of myself as you are. Better able, maybe."

"Aw, let her come, Matt," Tom protested. Tom was always agreeable. "Why not?"

"Because we don't want her. That's why not," Larry said flatly. Larry and Matt had been enemies when the state children had first come to the island. Then they had made up their quarrel, and now they always backed each other up in everything.

"That's right. You heard him, Sally. Come on, fellers." Matt started purposefully up the road, and the other two fell into step with him.

Sally stared balefully at the three retreating backs. Who did they think they were, trying to tell Sally Gray what she could and couldn't do? She'd show them. She started to follow them, keeping at a safe distance. If they wanted to be hateful, she could be hateful, too. She was well aware that simply by following them wherever. they went, she could spoil their whole morning. And it would serve them right.

For the first fifteen minutes or so, the boys ignored her. They led the way across the big field and into the woods that covered the crest of the island, talking among themselves and pausing occasionally to inspect a deer or rabbit track. Probably, Sally concluded, they thought she'd get tired of the game if they paid no attention to her. If so, they could think again. They didn't know old Super-Sally, the human bloodhound.

Besides, she had begun to enjoy herself. Not only was she getting even with the boys, a pleasure in itself, but the walk was fun. She had not been up here for a long time, and she had forgotten how nice it was. The tops of the trees tossed and glinted in the breeze, but down below, the air was quiet, stirred only faintly by the rumble of the Backside surf. The snow, dappled with a shifting pattern of light and shade, stretched clean and unmarked except for animal tracks in every direction. For a moment Sally considered giving up, and going on a private walk of her own. Everything was so peaceful and lovely here, it seemed almost a shame to waste the day on spitefulness.

The three boys suddenly broke into a run. So! They thought they could escape her that way, did they? Abandoning her better intentions abruptly, Sally started to run, too. She was the fastest runner on the island, as had been proved many times. That was one advantage of having long, skinny legs. She could run all three of them to a standstill if she had to, she was confident. This was becoming interesting.

The three boys, with Sally in hot pursuit, burst out of the shelter of the woods onto the windswept turf that crowned the ledges of the Backside. The sound of the surf was almost deafening, and Sally stopped short in awe. The whole length of the cobblestone beach below her was a smother of crashing green water, leaping spray, and blowing foam. She could see the great combers forming offshore, gathering size and speed as they neared the land, piling up one above the other, and tumbling in thunderous ruin onto the long curve of the beach. As each wave withdrew, there was a sighing sound and a faint, chimelike rattle of dislodged stones. Beyond the breakers, shining flights of gulls soared and then plummeted into the seething water after shoaling herring. It was a marvelous sight, Sally thought, worth crossing the island to see.

She brought her mind back to her true business here. The boys had gained a long lead while she had been watching the surf. Scrambling up like scalded cats, they were climbing the high outcropping of ledge that marked the farther limit of the beach. Their intention

was apparently to hide in the jumble of rocks beyond, where there was no snow to hold their footprints and reveal their whereabouts.

She'd see about that! She put on a burst of speed, her long legs eating up the distance, her red braids streaming out behind. She felt a surge of elation. This was almost like flying, with the wind and spray in her face and the glitter of sea and sky all around her. This must be how a sea gull felt.

Then a round stone rolled under her foot. She felt a stab of pain in her ankle, and found herself sprawled on the ground.

Some sea gull, she thought disgustedly, and sat up, testing her ankle gingerly. It hurt and she sat there for a minute, rubbing it. Gradually the pain subsided, so she guessed that nothing was broken.

Her pursuit of the boys was ended. She'd be lucky if she could get home unaided. She could call the boys and ask them to help her, but she'd be darned if she would. Even if they heard her over the roar of the sea, they would probably think it was a trick and stay in hiding. If they did come to her assistance, she would never hear the end of it. There would be all kinds of We-told-you-so's and Serves-you-right's. Though she really couldn't blame them if they crowed a little, she could do nicely without it. She would get home under her own steam, thank you.

She stood up slowly and tested her ankle again. Stepping on it was painful, but not unbearable. She found a good straight piece of driftwood to serve as a cane and started hopping and hobbling on the homeward path.

It was well past noon when she reached the village. Her progress had been slow, and she had been forced to sit down and rest now and then. By the time she opened the kitchen door her ankle was swollen and throbbing.

"You're late," Rhoda greeted her. "I've been waiting —" Then she saw Sally's white face. "What's the matter?" she asked in alarm. "Are you hurt?"

"Just turned my ankle." Sally sat down with a gasp. "It's nothing." She tried to pull off her boot.

Rhoda flew to her aid. "My land!" she exclaimed, examining the swollen ankle, "you sure made a job of it." She probed and poked with expert fingers. "Nothing's busted. Just a sprain. Soaking in hot water's the best thing."

She bustled efficiently around, filling a bucket with hot water, removing Sally's sock, settling her in a low chair with her foot in the pail.

"There," she said finally, "that'll do the trick. You'd best keep off it for the rest of the day." She paused, remembering something. "I was going to ask you to run down to the store for me. I'm clean out of baking powder and I've got my cake all stirred up except for that. Well, there's no help for it. You can't go, so I'll have to go myself." She started putting on her coat. "You keep a snug watch on Benjie. Now you hear me. I won't be gone long."

"Oh, take your time, Rhoda," Sally said expansively. Her foot felt better, and her spirits were rising. "I've still got one good leg under me, so you don't have to worry about a thing. Have a ball."

"I don't know's I'll go that far," Rhoda said, "but I'll admit it'll be good to get out of the house for a spell. You can take your foot out of that water as soon's it gets cold." She made sure that Benjie was secure in his chair, smoothed his hair, and was gone.

Sally watched her head bob past the window. She realized with a start that Benjie's head was turning ever so slightly in the direction Rhoda had taken. He *was* beginning to notice things. She had been pretty sure before, when he'd watched the birds, and now she was positive.

It was funny that Rhoda hadn't mentioned it. Surely she must have seen. She was with him all the time. Maybe that was the trouble. Maybe she was with him too much, so she didn't notice little changes. Or maybe Miss Bridges was right. Maybe Rhoda smothered Benjie with too much attention, preventing him from reacting.

Maybe's weren't important, though. She couldn't sit here maybe-ing all afternoon. She took her foot from the water and cautiously drew on her sock. Hopping across the floor, she turned Benjie's chair so that it faced the room. Then she looked about for something bright. Ben's blaze-orange hunting cap would do. She hopped to fetch it from where it hung beside the door, and waved it in a slow arc across Benjie's fixed gaze.

Nothing happened. Sally and the cap might have been invisible, for all the interest Benjie showed. Her heart sank. She had been so sure. She felt like shaking Benjie.

She shouldn't even be thinking such a thing. She should be considering some other way to get Benjie's attention. This was the first time she had been alone with him for more than a few minutes, and she had better make the most of it. She had seen him display interest twice. She was certain of that. Both times—

Of course! On neither occasion had anybody been paying any attention to him at all. She had thought of him once as a house where nobody lived. Now she believed that somebody did live there—a frightened somebody, in hiding. Naturally he wasn't going to give himself away when anybody was looking. The thing to do was to outwit him, to pretend that she couldn't care less whether he came out or not.

That shouldn't be hard. She didn't care. He wasn't her problem.

"Be stubborn if you want to," she told him aloud. "I don't care. You're not my problem."

That wasn't true, she realized immediately. He had spoiled things for her here with Ben and Rhoda. Unless he either changed or was taken away, he would go right on spoiling them. So he was her problem and she did care, in a left-handed sort of way that was not to her credit.

She sat down at the table and started whistling "Yellow Bird." Whistling was her special accomplishment, and she put in all the trills, making a real production of it. Then she rolled Ben's gaudy cap into a ball and tossed it ceiling high in time with the tune, trying to catch it with first one hand and then the other. This was hard to do in rhythm, and for a few minutes she forgot about Benjie.

When she remembered and stole a sidelong glance at him, Benjie's eyes were following the bright, moving object. They really were. There was no mistake. In her excitement she missed the catch, and the improvised ball fell to the floor and rolled under the table.

Sally said, "Shucks," and favoring her sore ankle, crawled after it. It was then, when she was wedged among the table and chair legs, that Rhoda came home.

Sally felt the cold draft from the open door and heard the surprise in Rhoda's tone. "What in tunket are you doing under there? Oh, you've moved Benjie's chair!" Her voice rose. "Oh, Sally, can't I leave this house for one minute without—"

Sally emerged from under the table, her face a little flushed with her exertions. She was too excited to mind Rhoda's sharpness.

"Look, Rhoda, I've got something to show you."

Quickly she told about Benjie's interest in the birds and explained her experiment.

"And he really did notice," she concluded. "Stand quiet over there and watch."

But, although she whistled until her mouth was dry and tossed Ben's cap until it became a blur before her eyes, Benjie simply sat.

"It's no use," Rhoda said finally. "You just imagined the whole thing."

"No! He did notice! I wasn't imagining it! Don't you believe me?"

Rhoda sighed and moved over to Benjie's side. "I want to believe you more than anything in the world"—she laid her cheek against Benjie's—"but sometimes we see things that aren't there, just because we want so terribly to see them. I know. It's almost happened to me a few times. It's what happened to you."

There was no use in arguing, Sally decided. Rhoda would not be convinced. But that didn't change the facts. Benjie had responded, no matter what Rhoda said.

CHAPTER 8

All through February the islanders had been saying that the weather was too good to last. "We're overdue for a change," they said, and, "When she comes, she'll be a real ripsnorter." Finally, early in March, their predictions came true.

Sally woke in the morning to the howl of rising winds, the crash of surf on the offshore reefs, and the rattle of wind-driven sleet against the window. She went down to the kitchen to find Ben still at home. Obviously none of the lobstermen would leave the harbor today. Having Ben there made it seem like a holiday, and Sally prepared to enjoy it.

After breakfast, however, Ben rose and started pulling on his boots. "Lots of work waiting for me down to the shop," he said, "and sitting here ain't going to get it done. Want to put me up a mug-up, Rhody?" A mug-up was a picnic lunch. "No sense in coming home in all this. Look alive, Sally, and I'll walk you down to school."

"School?" Sally was outraged. She looked out the window, where nothing could be seen except the tossing lilac bush against a background of wildly eddying fog and sleet. On the mainland, with its problems of icy roads and school buses, this would be a certain-sure no-school day. She said so indignantly.

"That may be." Ben was unimpressed. "Always did think they were a spleeny lot over on the main. We figure island children to be built to stand up to island weather, else they got no business here."

Sally was uncertain whether or not this was a hint that she was spleeny. She decided not to ask, and began bundling into heavy clothing. Protesting about school had only been a matter of habit, anyhow. Actually she would rather be there with the other kids than stormbound here with Rhoda and that Benjie.

When she and Ben stepped out into the blizzard, the wind almost took their breath away. Ben said something, and pointed. A little downy woodpecker, its scarlet cap bright, was clinging to one of the suet bags that Sally had hung in the lilac. The bag was blown out almost straight by the gale, and the bird's feathers were disheveled, but it pecked away composedly.

Ben put his lips close to Sally's ear. "Spunky little devil, ain't he?" he shouted, and waved to attract Rhoda's attention to the woodpecker. She was watching them from behind Benjie. She smiled and nodded. Benjie was as stolid as always.

That reminded Sally of something. She had never told Ben about Benjie and the birds. She never saw him alone long enough to have any lengthy discussions with him. Now might be the time.

But before she could speak, Linda came slithering and sliding out of her yard. "Oh, boy," she shouted. "I'm about to blow clean away."

Ben laughed. "The way it's making up, the whole island seems likely to slip her moorings. It ain't never yet in the past thousand years, but there's always a first time." He locked Sally's and Linda's arms firmly in his and bent into the storm. "I'll land you safe at school, never fear."

Sally shrugged within her heavy clothing. There went her chance to talk with Ben. Well, it probably didn't make any difference. He probably wouldn't have believed her anyhow, any more than Rhoda had.

There were no absences that morning. All eleven pupils were present, exhilarated by the fierceness of the storm. Even Miss Mills seemed to have caught the general holiday spirit. She was cheery as she helped the smaller children out of their wet wraps and hung the garments near the stove to dry.

"We'll have one session today," she announced. "There's no need of everybody's getting soaked twice. First, we'll all get right down to business and finish our lessons quickly. Then we'll clean house. After that, perhaps we'll have time for a game or two."

For a while it was quiet in the little building. Outside, the storm raged, rattling the doors and hurling a mixture of snow and sleet to blind the windows. Within was a pool of calm beneath the uproar. Heads were bent attentively over desks, and hands were raised obediently in response to questions. When Miss Mills said business, she meant business. Even when the schoolhouse shuddered under an unusually heavy blast, no one did more than glance up briefly.

Finally Miss Mills was satisfied with the morning's work. "Now we'll tidy our desks. I want every desk as neat as a pin before we leave. When you're ready for inspection, raise your hands."

Little Tony's was the first hand up, and he was allowed to pass the wastebasket for discarded papers. He walked up and down the aisles, solemn and pleased with his responsibility. Linda and Tom were next, and they were put to washing the blackboards. Ethel was given the task of watering Miss Mills's cherished geraniums. Sally and Matt were assigned to sweeping the floor, and Jenny was handed a duster. Everybody worked diligently, and soon the room was a model of order and cleanliness.

"Good," said Miss Mills. "We have time for a few games. Let's start with pass-the-eraser."

When the games ended with a spelling bee and school had been dismissed, Sally found herself reluctant to go home. Compared with the companionship and orderly activity of the morning, the prospect of spending a long, dull afternoon with Rhoda and Benjie was unattractive. Maybe Rhoda would help her make fudge or something;

but then again, maybe she wouldn't. Sally could go over to Linda's, she supposed, but being cooped up in the Allen house was not very appealing, either. She stood undecided on the schoolhouse steps, watching the snow stream across the yard.

"Come on, come on," Linda called impatiently from the road. "You going to stand there all day?"

Sally made up her mind. This would be a good time to talk with Ben. He had taken his lunch, so he would still be in his shop. She knew that the men visited back and forth along the waterfront, but maybe Ben would be alone. If he wasn't she would take it for a sign, and go home.

"You coming?" Linda called again. She was stamping her feet against the cold.

"You go on. I've got an errand—" Sally started loping down the road, hoping that Linda would not follow. After a minute, she looked back warily. All she saw was fog and snow. Linda had evidently decided to go home.

The harbor was veiled in falling snow through which a few ghostly lobster boats could be seen tugging at their moorings. The gulls, disconsolate, huddled in the shelter of the wharfs. Ben's shop was a faint gray shape with woodsmoke blowing flat from the chimney, and the light of kerosene lanterns showing golden at the little windows. Sally put her hand on the latch and literally blew in on a gust of wind and snow. She struggled to close the door against the gale and, slightly out of breath, turned to face the room.

Ben was alone, eating a sandwich and drinking a cup of coffee from the smoke-streaked coffeepot that stood perpetually on the potbellied wood stove.

"Well!" he exclaimed. "This is a nice surprise. Here, sit down and have a sandwich. There's plenty. You know Rhody. I'm glad to have company. I was beginning to talk to myself for want of anyone better."

Sally sat down on an upturned nail keg and looked around. It was warm and cozy in here, like a dim cave filled with the smell of paint, new wood, tar, woodsmoke, and the sea. The splash and gurgle of water came up through the floor, which was built out over the shelving beach, and the wind whooped and whuffled over the roof. It was a good comfortable place in which to have a private chat.

"Is this just a neighborly visit," Ben asked after a moment, "or have you got something special on your mind?"

"Yes, I have." She might just as well come right to the point. "It's about Benjie. It's none of my business, but there's some things you ought to know." She went on to tell him about the birds and the game she had played with his cap on the day when she had sprained her ankle. The story came out in a rush, once she was started.

"Rhoda won't believe me," she concluded. "Benjie never does these things when she's around, and she thinks I'm making it all up. Maybe you won't believe me either, Ben, but I know what I saw. I wouldn't lie about a thing like this. You know that, Ben."

Ben looked at her searchingly. "Yup," he said, "I cal'-

78

late I do know it." He fell silent, twirling his coffee cup around on his finger by the handle and staring out the snow-veiled window. Finally he said, "I sure hope to Hannah you're right. What you say you saw don't sound like much, but it's a lot, considering. Benjie's been here two months, and I'd about given up hoping. I guess the question now is, what do we do next?"

Probably Ben was going to be mad at what she had to say. She felt like a sneak, talking about Rhoda behind her back. But that could not be helped. She had started this, and she had to finish it. "If Rhoda would loosen up on Benjie a little, sort of let go— Ben, I'm not saying anything against Rhoda. She's doing what she thinks is right. Maybe she is right. She's older and smarter than I am. But, she—well, Miss Bridges called it smothering him, kind of."

"Ayuh, I know what you mean," Ben admitted, not mad at all. He added rather surprisingly, "The way she hovers over him is enough to give anyone the fidgets." He put down his coffee cup, picked up a brush, and started painting a lobster buoy. "I'll talk to her. I know you've offered to help and she wouldn't let you. Being with you more couldn't do Benjie any harm, leastwise not that I can see, and it just might do some good. I'll talk to her, anyhow."

Ben was as good as his word. Long after she had gone to bed that night, Sally could hear his and Rhoda's voices running on beneath the diminishing sounds of the storm. When Sally came down to a crystal-clear, diamond-bright, blue-and-white morning, Rhoda said a little self-consciously, "Are you planning on coming straight home from school? Because if you are, I thought of running up to Emma's for a spell this afternoon. She's piecing a new quilt pattern I'd admire to see, and if you could sit with Benjie—"

Sally smiled inwardly. Good for old Ben. For all his easygoing nature, he knew how to put his foot down when he had to. Demurely she told Rhoda that yes, she was planning to come straight home from school.

Things changed a little after that. Often, after school, Rhoda left Benjie in Sally's care while she dropped in at a neighbor's or went down to the store. Sometimes Sally found this a nuisance, but she reminded herself that she had asked for it. She was in no position to complain. Besides, the change in Rhoda made it worthwhile. She began to be something like her old self, now that she was resuming her old life.

As the days grew longer and the sun warmer, Sally started to take Benjie on little walks around the yard and along the road. Usually Linda was with them. Benjie would go anywhere, as long as someone led him by the hand. Left alone, he simply stopped walking and stood still until someone set him in motion again. But Sally was sure that he noticed things that went on around him. One day when the Chandlers' big black dog came charging down the hill, she was sure that he drew back a little. Linda said she imagined it. But Linda, Sally reflected, didn't know Benjie as well as she did. Linda couldn't be expected to notice small differences in his behavior.

Linda was the one, however, who stopped short one day with a surprised "Hey!" The two girls were walking along with Benjie between them, swinging his hands in time with a song they were singing. Unconsciously and naturally, they were marching in time with the tune.

"Hey," Linda said again, "Benjie's walking in step with us."

They began singing and marching again. Sure enough, Benjie's steps matched theirs.

"Let's try something else." Sally was excited. "Let's try 'When Johnny Comes Marching Home.'"

It worked. Benjie did really hear and heed the music. At last here was something that even Rhoda could see and, seeing, would have to believe. With a hasty "Hold everything" to Linda, Sally dropped Benjie's hand and ran into the house.

With Rhoda standing motionless on the doorstep, they tried it again. "John Brown's body lies a-mouldering in the grave," they caroled, stamping their feet and swinging Benjie's hands smartly to emphasize the beat. Again Benjie marched in perfect step with them, in striking contrast to his usual aimless gait.

"See, Rhoda?" Sally cried. "He's keeping time."

Rhoda shook her head. "I don't see that he's got much choice, the way you two are yanking on his arms," she said dryly. "Anything else would land him flat on his face."

Sally stopped, exasperated. Rhoda just did not want to believe, or maybe she was afraid to. For a moment, Sally and Linda stood there with Benjie between them, looking up at Rhoda, trying to think of some way to convince her.

Then, with no word from anyone, Benjie tugged at the girls' hands, leaning forward and stamping his feet. He liked marching, he was saying in the only way he could. He wanted to march some more.

Rhoda's eyes widened for a startled second. Her face crumpled. With a strangled sob, she flung herself down the steps to gather all three children in a tight embrace.

At last, Rhoda was convinced.

CHAPTER 9

Something woke Sally one night. She sat up and peered out the window beside her bed. Over a year ago, when she was new on the island, she had once looked out this window in the middle of the night and seen a fox. It had been a cold, clear, silent night, and the ground had been covered with frost that shone like silver in the moonlight. And there, walking slowly through the yard, had been the fox. He had looked black against the glitter, and wild and lordly. He had sat down on the ledge at the edge of the little lawn and gazed out over the village and harbor as though he owned them. The frost-light had glinted on his fur and turned his eyes to fire. Sally had fallen in love with him on sight, he looked so independent and self-possessed and free. She kept hoping she would see him again, but she never had.

Tonight there was no fox and no moon. Everything was black out there except for a streak of starlight on the sea. Starhaven had no streetlights, and all the houses that she could see were dark and quiet. After a moment, she

❧ 84

lay back on the pillow. But sleep eluded her. She started thinking about Benjie.

He had come a long way in the past month, she thought with satisfaction. He noticed lots of things now. He almost smiled when something pleased him, and his face puckered up in a frown when he was unhappy. He really seemed to enjoy his walks, as nearly as anyone could tell. She wished he would have ideas of his own, instead of obediently following someone else's lead; and she wished he would begin to talk. Even one word—

She stiffened at a small sound, and then relaxed. Rhoda or Ben was coming upstairs. It couldn't be as late as she had thought, or they wouldn't still be prowling around the house. She drifted off to sleep.

When she woke again, the sun was shining and she could hear Ben talking in the kitchen. He was late this morning, she thought as she dressed. Lobstermen usually put out to sea at the first glimmer of dawn. She went downstairs and stopped short at the kitchen door, staring. Rhoda was pacing the floor, her face swollen and her eyes red with sleeplessness and pain.

"She's been up all night with this toothache," Ben explained. "I'm going to take her over to the main, soon's the dentist's office is open. You'll have to tend to things here."

"Sure," Sally said. "I'm sorry, Rhoda."

Rhoda tried to smile. "I'm afraid it'll mean missing school today, but I don't know of anyone else I'd trust

Benjie to." Her words came out oddly from her distorted face. "We'll stop by and let Miss Mills know. You *will* take good care of him, won't you?"

"Absolutely the best," Sally promised. "You just worry about yourself. Don't give us a thought."

After Ben and Rhoda had gone, Sally busied herself around the house. She dressed Benjie and gave him his breakfast, trying to make him feed himself as much as possible. With a little prodding and urging, he did not do too badly.

She felt very competent and a little bit smug as she watched the other children pass on their way to school. She had more important things to do today. She would mop the kitchen floor, wash out a few towels and pillow-cases, and do a little cooking. There were some fresh clams in the cellarway. She would have a good hot clam chowder all ready when Ben and Rhoda got home, and maybe she would try her hand at cookies. She had watched Rhoda often enough. She ought to be able to set a good meal on the table. Housekeeping was fun, when you were your own boss and could make your own plans.

The morning passed swiftly, but after Sally had fed Benjie his dinner and laid him down for his nap, time began to drag a little. What did Rhoda do with herself at this slack time of day? Sally's eye fell on Rhoda's basket, heaped with Ben's socks. Rhoda did the mending in the afternoon, she remembered. She sat down in

Rhoda's low rocking chair, threaded a needle with gray yarn, and picked up a sock.

It was not as easy as it looked when Rhoda did it. Sally crisscrossed a large hole with yarn and, tongue protruding from the corner of her mouth in concentration, began weaving the needle in and out in the other direction. When she had finished, she inspected her handiwork. It looked terrible—all bunchy and rough instead of smooth and neat, like Rhoda's. If Ben tried to wear this sock, he would have a blister on his heel as big as a walnut. Sighing, she ripped out what she had done. She would be glad when school was out and Linda came over. Benjie would be awake then, and they could take him for a walk.

After school the entire student body trailed into the Coopers' yard. The day had turned springlike, warm and balmy, for the first time since last fall. Everybody was a little restless. Someone had suggested a game of hare and hounds, and everybody else had fallen in eagerly with the idea. It offered some excitement and a chance to work off stored-up energy. Matt was one captain, and Linda the other, they told Sally. Matt had won the toss-up, and his first choice was Sally, because she could run the fastest.

Sally was flattered. She would have expected Matt to choose his bosom pal, Larry. Her eyes brightened. After her quiet day it would be wonderful to race through the woods, laying a deceptive trail of paper scraps, doubling back to outwit the pursuers. Then she remembered.

"I can't," she said regretfully. "Ben and Rhoda aren't back yet, and I've got to take care of Benjie."

Matt's face fell. "Can't you tie him in a chair or something, and leave him? Nothing would happen to him."

"Don't be a chowderhead. Of course I can't." Sally was cross because she wanted so much to join the game.

"Darn Benjie, anyhow," Matt said. "He's a pain in the neck."

Sally flew at him, her fists clenched. "You take that back, Matt Cole," she spat. "You ought to be ashamed of yourself. Poor little kid, he can't help it. You take back what you said, or I'll—I'll—" She hit him as hard as she could, and then hit him again. The sting of the blows filled her with satisfaction.

"Hey!" Matt backed off, arms raised to protect his face. "Take it easy. I didn't mean to ruffle your feathers. I take it back. Benjie's not a pain in the neck. That satisfy you?" He was laughing a little at her fierceness.

Sally's rage subsided. She didn't know why she had lost her temper in the first place. Matt had only said what she herself had thought plenty of times in the past few months. She looked at Benjie, standing there so helpless and good, patiently waiting to be taken on his walk.

"Never you mind, Benjie," she said. "Sally doesn't think you're a pest."

The minute she said it, she realized with surprise that it was true. Somewhere along the line, though she did not know exactly when, she had stopped resenting Benjie and had begun really to care about him. She took his hand in hers.

"Phooey to the whole bunch of them," she told him. "We'll find something better to do."

"Gee, Sally, I'd come with you," Linda began apologetically, "only I'm captain. You won't be mad at me?"

"It's okay, Linda. I'm not mad." Yesterday she might have been, she thought, but today she wasn't. Yesterday Benjie was a nuisance, but today he was somebody who depended on her. She watched the others move off up the road. "Have fun," she called after them, meaning it.

Now, where would she and Benjie go? She looked around for inspiration. Smoke was rising from the chimney of a small house on the farther side of the harbor. Old Perley Stevens must be at home. She and Benjie would go over and visit with him. It wasn't too far for Benjie to walk, and old Perley was always glad to have company.

Nobody, not even he himself, knew exactly how old Perley was. He had been born on the island and had lived there all his life, lobstering from the time he was eight until he reached his eighties. Then he had sold his boat and retired to the shore. He had never married. He lived alone in the house in which he had been born, and his parents and grandparents before him. He was one of the busiest men on the island. He dug clams, caught a few fish for his own use, cultivated a large vegetable garden, kept his house in apple-pie order, and lent a hand to the other men in painting boats and repairing gear as the need arose. People said that he knew more about winds and tides and shoals and currents than any other man on the coast of Maine. They were probably right.

Today, when Sally knocked at his door, Perley was sitting in his kitchen knitting a sock. "Come in, come in. It ain't fastened," he called. His bright old eyes lighted as they entered. "Well, now, this is a real pleasure. Lay off your wraps and set a spell. I'll brew us up a dish of tea."

Sally said no-thank-you to the tea, removed Benjie's coat, and settled him in a chair. Then she took off her own jacket and prepared to listen. Perley, like many people who live alone, made up for lost time when he found someone to talk to.

"When I was a young one," he started in, "they give us tea the minute we was weaned. Nowadays they claim it stunts the growth and rots the brains. Man and boy, I've drunk enough tea to float a battleship, and been none the worse for it. I heartily recommend it for whatever may ail a body. Howsomever, if you won't, you won't. How about one of my hermits? I baked off a batch this morning, and if I do say so as shouldn't, you'd travel a good day's journey to beat them."

Sally said she would love a hermit. Perley put down his knitting and rose to take a pink-flowered plate from the cupboard over the sink. As he crossed the floor a little tortoiseshell kitten came out from under the stove, blinking and yawning and stretching its tiny paws.

Sally exclaimed delightedly, "Oh, isn't he darling! I didn't know you had a kitten, Perley."

"I didn't till a short while ago. Then my old Samanthy presented me with a litter. I was some old surprised. I thought she was too old for that nonsense." He filled the plate with moist, dark, raisin-filled hermits and placed it on the table. "Help yourself. Four of them," he continued, going back to Samanthy's litter, "and I tell you, they keep me and Sam hopping. Here, I'll roust out the rest of them for you to look at."

He prodded gently under the stove with a broom, and three more kittens came tumbling and staggering into the open. Two of them were tortoiseshell, but the last was the queerest-looking cat that Sally had ever seen. It had no tail at all and hopped like a rabbit when it moved. Its short, almost velvety, fur was mixed and mottled, mostly dark brown, but splashed and spotted with orange, black, tan, and white. Because of the irregular marking, its little triangular face looked lopsided.

"Now ain't she the downright homeliest object you ever see in all your born days?" Perley demanded admiringly. "I've seen some funny-looking cats in my time, but she's the limit. The others, now, they're real handsome. They favor their mother. I guess the makings run out when it come to this one. She's a real smart, biddable little thing, though." It was plain to see that he was proud of his odd kitten. "Real knowing and quick to learn."

"What kind of cat is she?" Sally wanted to know.

"She's a money cat. Ain't you never seen one before? I've heard tell that Maine's the only place that has them, though I wouldn't take oath to it. Some folks say they're called money cats because the spots on them look like coins, and some say it's because a he money cat would be worth a fortune. They're most always she-cats. Here, give the boy a hermit."

Sally put a piece of cooky in Benjie's hand and started him eating it. When he seemed ready to proceed on his own, she asked, "Don't money cats ever have tails?"

"Mostly. But this one's got some Manx blood in her somewheres, and maybe a little Siamese, judging by her actions. We've got some pretty fancy cat mixtures here in Maine. It goes back to sailing days, when the clipper ships was scurrying round all over the globe. The crews would bring back these outlandish cats to their wives as curiosities. Persians, Burmese, Angoras, Manx, I don't know what-all. As the years went by, they crossbred, and once in a while an old strain will crop out." He changed the subject. "What's new over on the other side of the harbor?"

"Well, Rhoda's got a toothache, so Ben's taken her over to the main—"

"I surmised something like that, when I see Ben's boat put out this morning. I said to myself at the time, 'Perley,' I said—" He was off again. He asked questions, Sally decided, chiefly to provide himself with new topics of conversation. She settled back to listen.

Perley was well into a hair-raising account of his experiences with a dentist up at Portland when Sally sat up abruptly. She had not been paying any attention to Benjie, knowing that he would stay where she had seated him until she stood him on his feet.

Now he was climbing out of his chair—Benjie, who never, *never* did anything on his own.

Sally choked back an exclamation and controlled her impulse to jump up. "Go on talking, Perley," she begged silently. "Just keep right on talking." She forced herself to sit still, not even turning her head in Benjie's direction, watching only out of the corners of her eyes.

Slowly but easily, Benjie lowered himself to the floor and stood for a second, as though surprised at himself. Then, hands outstretched, he started across the floor. He seemed to know exactly what he was doing—to have some definite object in mind.

Sally's eyes slid further around. Over by the woodbox, the little money cat was playing with a small piece of bark, batting it delicately with a tiny paw, crouching, springing onto it, tossing it into the air. The cat was so absorbed that it did not notice Benjie until he was almost within touching distance. Then it arched its back, its fur standing on end, and hissed.

Sally jumped up, but Perley said quietly, "Rest easy. Leave them alone."

"They'll hurt each other. Benjie's never—Perley, Benjie's never done anything—not anything at all."

"I know, I know." Old Perley knew everything that happened on the island. "He's backward." Sally guessed

🌱 93

that was as good a word as any for Benjie. "It happens sometimes. But it might be he's getting ready for a forward step."

The kitten, its back still arched and its eyes round, was retreating slowly behind the woodbox. Suddenly it whirled and was gone. Benjie tried to follow, bumped his head hard, and howled. Sally had never heard him make such a racket before. She picked him up and patted him soothingly, but he squirmed and reached in the direction the kitten had taken.

"There, there," Perley said. With the broom he eased the kitten out from its hiding place, picked it up, and placed it on the table. "Easy now," he said to Benjie. "Stroke the nice kitty. Easy, easy, that's the ticket."

Benjie's hand went out and rested on the silky fur. Then he laughed—a real out-loud laugh, the first of his whole life. Sally looked at Perley. She wanted to say something, but was surprised to find that she could not speak. Her throat felt all closed up.

"Well, now, don't that take the cake!" Perley was never out of words. "Looks like he's got a real way with critters. Some folks do have. They steer clear of their own kind, but when it comes to something with fur or feathers on it, they're right in their element. See how the little kitty's simmering down. She knows who likes her."

Sure enough, the money cat was purring and lifting her head to Benjie's hand. Her eyes were half closed with pleasure.

Perley was suddenly businesslike. "I've a good mind to

give you that kitten. It's time I was finding homes for the litter anyhow. They're weaned and housebroke, and Samanthy and I are about due to get back to normal. We're both too old to put up with young-ones' shenanigans. I've got a box here somewheres, just about the right size for a kitten."

Sally found her voice. "Oh, I'd love to have the kitten, but maybe I'd better ask Rhoda first. She might not—"

"Don't you fret none about Rhody. Benjie here's been a cross and a worriment for her to bear, don't think I don't know that. When she sees how the two of them take to each other—Well, you won't have no trouble with Rhody, that I'll guarantee you."

Perley was probably right, Sally thought with relief. She really did want the kitten. It was such a laughable little thing with its crooked face and tailless, bobbing, rounded rump. Rhoda would let her keep it, if only for Benjie's sake.

"Has she got a name?" she asked.

"Well, I've been calling her Ree-ject, on account of the way she looks—like something off a bargain counter," Perley admitted.

"*Ree-ject!*" Sally was shocked. "Perley, that's terrible. She's got enough going against her without reminding her all the time how ugly she is. She ought to have a name like Princess or Beauty or—"

Perley shrugged. "You can suit yourself, of course. She's your cat now. Me, I cal'late it's best to know what you are and learn to live with it. Ree-ject ain't never going to get no blue ribbons on looks, and she might as well face up to it. But go ahead and name her Sheba or Gloria or anything else you see fit. It's your say-so now."

Walking home with Benjie, the kitten in a box under her arm, Sally thought over what Perley had said. Maybe he was right. Maybe it was best not to try to fool yourself about yourself.

"Benjie," she said aloud, "we're three of a kind. I'm a State Kid that nobody wanted, and you're backward, and Ree-ject's the homeliest cat in Maine. We're a fine bunch of no-bargains. But maybe if we all stick together, we'll make out all right."

CHAPTER 10

As Perley had foreseen, Rhoda made no real objection to the adoption of Ree-ject. She said something about Benjie's getting scratched, and added something about its seeming very funny to her that, with all the pretty kittens in the world, they got stuck with one homely enough to stop a clock. But her heart wasn't in it. Sally decided that Rhoda's face hurt too much for her to take an interest in any kitten right then.

It turned out that Rhoda had more on her mind than her sore tooth. While in Stillport, she and Ben had stopped at the post office and picked up the mail, which usually was sent over on the ferry twice a week. Among the slim packet of letters for island families was one from Nathan and Laurel, announcing their intention of spending Easter weekend on the island. The girls would be having their spring vacation from school, and Nathan would be able to take Friday off from work. They would arrive on Friday afternoon and stay until Sunday morning.

"When I read that letter," Rhoda told Sally, "it did

me more good than a dozen dentists. Imagine! They'll be here a week from Friday. It's been longer than I care to think about since Nathan's spent a night under this roof. I just hope the weather holds good for them. Not that Nathan would mind. He's island born and bred. But for the sake of the others— I'll plan on a good pot of home-baked beans and brown bread for Saturday, and Friday night I'll—"

"Whoa!" Ben laughed. Though he didn't say much, Sally could see that he was as pleased as Rhoda was. "You've got eight or nine days to plan meals. It don't have to be done all of a minute. Right now the rest of those letters had better be delivered. Other folks may have good news waiting to be read. You want to take them around, Sally?"

"Sure." Sally felt a little let down. She hadn't had a chance to get a word in edgewise. She was bursting to tell about Benjie's behavior with Ree-ject, but you couldn't just toss a thing like that into a conversation as though it were nothing. You had to *tell* it. She had hoped actually to show Ben and Rhoda how Benjie responded to the kitten.

Oh, well, all that could wait until Rhoda simmered down. Rhoda and Ree-ject. Right now the kitten was hiding under the stove, wary of the strange surroundings and in no mood to be shown off. There would be plenty of time later, when things were calmer.

Ree-ject calmed down first. With the great composure of cats, she spent twenty-four hours exploring her new

❦ 99

home, prowling into odd corners and investigating un-accustomed sounds and smells. She tried out several chairs for size and comfort, ignoring the box that Sally had lined with an old sweater for her bed. She was slapped twice for jumping on the table and once for swinging on the kitchen curtains.

In spite of this, she decided to adopt the family as her own. She made it very clear that, while she would humor the rest of them in trivial matters like tables and curtains, otherwise she was boss. She chose Rhoda's mending basket as the best place to sleep, and the windowsill by Benjie's chair as an observation post. From it she could see everyone passing on the road and watch the birds coming and going around the feeder. Ree-ject plainly liked to keep track of things.

Benjie followed her around like a shadow, picking her up whenever he could catch her. He was remarkably gentle with her. At first she struggled to be free, but almost immediately she accepted his attentions as one of the things she was going to have to put up with. She was, as Perley had said, a real smart, biddable little thing, for all her peculiar appearance. "Biddable," Sally con-cluded, was the same thing as "adjustable."

"I never," Rhoda said, "never in my born days, saw anything like it." She was between laughing and crying. "It's like a miracle. To think that after all the doctors and specialists and schools, a foolish little kitten without even a tail to bless itself with was the one to help Benjie. To see him running around like he knows what he's doing—

Well, I'll admit it now. I was getting discouraged. And just when Nathan and Laurel are coming, too. Now they'll have to admit we were right in taking Benjie."

"He's got a long way to go," Ben warned her. He was warning himself, too, Sally suspected. "Don't get your hopes up too high. He still don't talk and don't appear to listen. Maybe he never will."

Rhoda whirled on him. "Don't you say that, Ben Cooper! Of course he's got a long way to go. But he's made a start. That's the point. He's made a start!"

Between her excitement over Benjie and her preparations for the coming visit, Rhoda never did calm down completely. She made plans for meals and changed them daily, even hourly. She cleaned house furiously, determined that Laurel should find nothing to criticize. Dissatisfied with the appearance of Nathan's old room, she painted the woodwork. That, she decided, made the wallpaper look shabby in comparison, and she nagged at Ben to take her over to Stillport to buy some new.

"Nope," Ben refused flatly, "I ain't a-going to do it. Laurel's slept with that wallpaper before, and she'll survive it again. This house is tore up enough without you wearing yourself out hanging wallpaper. The way you're raring round, you'll be flat on your back in bed, plumb wore out, by the time they get here."

"No, I won't," Rhoda stated positively.

And she wasn't. When Good Friday finally arrived and it was time to go down to meet the boat, she was fresh as a daisy.

❧ 101

It had been decided not to take Benjie down to the harbor, for fear the confusion of first greetings would upset him. He and Sally would stay quietly at home and await the arrival of the family.

"I'm not going to say one word to them about Benjie's improvement," Rhoda told Sally. "When they ask, I'm just going to say, 'Oh, Benjie's fine.' They'll take that to mean that he's just the same as before. Then when they see how he trails that Ree-ject around— Well! I can't wait to see their faces!"

Things did not work out as she had planned, unfortunately. Ree-ject was sitting on her windowsill when the family came trooping into the yard. After one outraged glare at what appeared to be a hostile army she leaped from her perch and vanished up the steep, narrow stairs. Sally knew that was the last of Ree-ject for a while. She had hiding places up there that no one had yet been able to discover.

Benjie jumped down and started to follow Ree-ject. He was in the middle of the floor when the kitchen door burst open. Startled, he froze in his tracks. Then, when Laurel approached him with outstretched arms, his shoulders sagged a little. Sick at heart, Sally saw all the animation drain out of his face and the old, dull, glazed look shutter his eyes.

Laurel lifted him in her arms. "He's gained weight," she said. "You've taken good care of him, Mother Cooper." She was talking about him as though he were the old Benjie, the puppet Benjie.

Sally couldn't stand it. She burst out eagerly, "Just wait—"

Rhoda interrupted her, speaking more loudly than usual. "Ben, why don't you take the folks upstairs and show them where they're going to sleep? Maybe they might like to unpack while it's still light. Sally"—she put out a restraining hand as Sally started to help Tracy and Nan with their luggage—"you can help me down here."

As soon as they could hear the others tramping around over their heads, Rhoda said softly and urgently, "Don't tell them anything, Sally. Let them see for themselves."

"But maybe with them here, Benjie won't act like he's been doing. They ought to know, hadn't they, how much better—?"

"They wouldn't believe us. I wouldn't believe you, Sally, when you tried to tell me things about Benjie. They'd think I was making things up to prove that I was right in bringing him here. Seeing's believing. We've got to wait and see what happens."

The trouble was that nothing happened. When the others came downstairs, Benjie was staring dully out the window. At suppertime he refused to feed himself, and when it was time for him to go to bed, he was as limp and lifeless as a rag doll. Sally hadn't realized how much he had learned to help himself in eating and undressing until now, when he would not do either.

Saturday was a beautiful day. Far away to the west over the miles of blue water, the mountains of the mainland gleamed white and ghostly with snow, but out here on the island there was a hint of spring in the air. The island weather was always less extreme than that of the main. The surrounding ocean kept it warmer in winter, cooler in summer.

Ree-ject, Rhoda informed Sally when she came down for breakfast, had already eaten and gone outdoors. "Cats are all alike," Rhoda said. "Set in their ways. Independent, too. If things don't go to their liking, they wash their hands of the whole business. Ree-ject don't cotton to company, so she's lighted out. I'll have a thing or two to say to her when she gets back."

Sally laughed. She hoped she'd be present when Rhoda gave Ree-ject her talking-to. "Where's everybody else?" she asked.

"Oh, Nathan was up at first light to go out hauling with his father. The rest of them are still abed. You can get Benjie up and dressed, if you've a mind to. I'm hoping that today he'll—" She didn't have to finish the hope that Benjie would come out of his shell a little.

Later in the morning, Linda came over. Sally was glad to see her. She realized that Rhoda was depending on her to entertain Nan and Tracy, and she did not know quite what to do with them. After hearing their chatter about dancing classes, riding school, and the movies and parties they had attended, she felt that anything the island had to offer would seem pretty tame to them.

Linda had no such qualms. "Hey," she said, "my mother says she bets anything that the pussywillows are coming out up along the brook. Let's go see. We can take a bunch to Miss Mills on Monday. She really goes for things like that. What do you say?"

Laurel thought it was a good idea. "We can take some home. Pussywillows are something we don't have in the city. Yes, run along, girls. I'd like to have a talk with Mother Cooper anyhow."

"Well, what are we waiting for?" When Linda had an idea, she liked to put it into action immediately. "Come on. Where's Benjie's snowsuit?"

"Benjie's—? He's not going with us, is he?" Tracy sounded disgusted and disbelieving.

That did not disturb Linda. "Sure. Why not? He goes most places with Sally and me." She found the snowsuit and began stuffing Benjie into it. "Come on, Benjie, snap out of it. Don't act so helpless."

Laurel made a sound of protest, but Rhoda said, "It's all right, Laurel. Linda's used to Benjie, and he to her. They get along fine."

Laurel looked doubtful, but Linda briskly zipped Benjie up. "There," she said. "Let's go, everybody."

The four girls set off up the road with Benjie. It really did seem like spring, in spite of the remnants of snow still clinging in shaded places. The frozen ground was melting under the bright sun, and high overhead the gulls, who had stayed close to the harbor during the cold weather, were wheeling and soaring in shining spirals. Up ahead in the shelter of the woods, the fish crows and ravens were cawing and croaking in some sort of congress of their own. Long before the girls could see the brook, they could hear it—a light, chuckling sound in pleasant contrast to the slow, deep grumble of the surf. When they came out onto its banks, they found it swollen by the melting snow.

The lure of the running water was irresistible. Before they thought, the girls were throwing sticks into the stream, watching them spin and bob down the current.

"My boat won!" Nan crowed.

"It didn't either. We weren't even racing. Everybody find a boat and throw it in when I say *Go*." Tracy, Sally reflected, was like her mother, a great organizer. "Ready? All right. One, two, three—*Go!*"

The four sticks splashed into the water as one, and the four girls followed them downstream, each cheering her own entry in the race. It was fun. When everybody else's boats stranded on the banks, Linda was declared the winner.

"Let's do it again," Nan urged. "Everybody ready? One, two—"

"No. Wait." Sally looked back to a bend in the brook where Benjie was standing woodenly and forlornly alone. "Wait till I get Benjie. We can't leave him there."

"I didn't want to bring him in the first place. I knew he'd just be a bother and spoil everything." Tracy was smug. "It won't hurt him to stay there for a while. Come on. One, two—"

"Aw, Tracy," Linda interrupted. "It won't hurt us to wait a minute, either. Poor little Benjie—"

"Why don't you mind your own business, Linda

Whatever-your-name-is? He's not your brother. I guess I've got a right to say what my own brother—"

Sally turned on her. "You haven't any right at all, Tracy Cooper. Gee whiz! Benjie may be your brother, but every single person on this island cares more about him than you do. You don't—"

"You just wait." Tracy narrowed her eyes. "You wait till I tell my mother what you said. You take back every word of it, or I will tell her, and then you'll be sorry."

Sally drew a deep breath. If that stuck-up, la-di-da little snip wanted a fight, she had certainly come to the right place.

Behind Sally's back, Linda warned softly, "Take it

easy. She really might go tattling, and Rhoda'll nail you to the woodshed door. They're her family, after all."

Sally let her breath out slowly. Linda was right. Tracy was the grandchild, and Sally was only the State Kid who was supposed to be entertaining the visitors. Every word she had said was true, but that wouldn't matter. She had better apologize, although it would half kill her.

"I'm sorry," she muttered. Deep in her coat pockets, the fingers of both hands were crossed. She felt a little better for this secret, defiant gesture. It meant that what she said didn't count.

"Come on, let's play boats," Nan clamored.

But the fun had gone out of the game. After a few halfhearted races, Linda said that it was getting late, so they'd better pick their pussywillows and start home.

Sally could see, the minute that she entered the kitchen, that something was troubling Rhoda. She exclaimed just a little too enthusiastically over the pussywillows. She was just a little too breezy and cheerful. Her talk with Laurel had evidently disturbed her, though she was trying hard to act natural.

"Did you have a nice walk?" she asked Nan and Tracy.

Sally looked hard at Tracy, daring her to mention their quarrel, and Tracy said smoothly and very sweetly, "Very nice, thank you, Grandmother." So that was all right.

Rhoda turned to Sally, who was removing Benjie's

overshoes. "You didn't see anything of Ree-ject in your travels, did you?"

"Nope." Sally seated Benjie in his chair by the window. "But she'll show up. She's just nervous with so many people around. She'll come home when she gets hungry. She always does."

"I suppose so." Rhoda didn't seem very happy about it, and Sally glanced at her sharply. It wasn't like Rhoda to worry about Ree-ject. She was the one who always said cats could fend for themselves.

Rhoda dismissed the subject. "How would you girls like to dye Easter eggs after dinner? The old-fashioned way, like we used to do when I was a young one?" She rattled on about beet juice and onion skins and decorating the eggs, and the kitten was forgotten.

Later, though, when Sally went out to fill the feeder for the birds' evening meal, Rhoda joined her. The others were absorbed in their egg decorating. Rhoda said loudly, as she stepped out, "We won't be using that much longer, what with spring nearly here and plenty of other food for the birds."

"Can't we leave it up? I know the birds won't need it, but Benjie loves watching—"

Rhoda closed the door behind her and moved close to Sally. "Of course we'll leave it up. I only said that for their benefit." She nodded toward the house. Then her voice became urgent. "Look, Sally, we've got to find Ree-ject. While you girls were gone this morning, Laurel told me that she'd talked Nathan into agreeing to take Benjie away and place him in that school, if he hadn't shown any improvement here. We know how he's come along in the past weeks, but the way he's acted since they've been here—"

Sally was aghast. "They can't take him away! Why, he's improving all the time. Didn't you tell Laurel?"

"I told her, but like I expected, she didn't believe me. I can't blame her, really." Rhoda was trying to be fair. "The things I told her would be hard for her to believe, considering what she's been seeing since she's been here. She feels that she's given us a chance with Benjie, and we failed, so now she'll give the school a chance. I suppose she has to. Benjie's her child."

"She might believe me. I've got no reason for lying. Benjie's nothing to me."

Sally stopped short, shocked by her own words. Benjie was a lot to her, she realized. She did not have time now to wonder when or how this had come about. She only knew that she could not stand it if Nathan and Laurel took Benjie away.

"What are we going to do?" she asked despairingly.

"We've got to find Ree-ject. She's our last hope. If anything will bring Benjie out of this slump, it'll be that cat." Rhoda peered around the yard and began calling, "Here, kit-kit-kit, here, kitty, kit-kit," in the coaxing tone that usually brought Ree-ject running. But no kitten came rabbit-hopping out of the bushes.

"I'll look around the neighborhood for her," Sally offered. "I'll get Linda to help."

But though they combed the village until after dark and called and called until they were hoarse, they saw nothing of Ree-ject. Like all cats, she did exactly as she pleased, and she did not please to come home to a houseful of strangers. She was probably, Linda told Sally, right near at hand, watching them and listening to them and laughing at them.

She still had not come back by morning. Sally got up early and scouted around, but nobody had seen Ree-ject. She trailed back to the house, discouraged, to find the others up and dressed and ready for breakfast. Ben had not gone out hauling, since he was going to take the younger Coopers over to Stillport after they had eaten. He stood talking with Nathan, waiting for Rhoda to call them to the table.

Sally heard the tail end of the conversation as she came in the door. Nathan would make arrangements with the school as soon as he got back to Boston, and the next time he came to the island, it would be to get Benjie. Sally felt sick. If they would only *listen*.

Rhoda turned the last crisp pancake and placed it on the heaping platter. "All ready," she announced, trying to sound matter-of-fact. "Sit down, everybody, and pitch in while they're hot. No, Sally, never mind Benjie. I gave him his breakfast earlier." Her tone told Sally that she had given up hoping. Since Benjie was simply going to sit, he might just as well sit by his window.

It was not a very cheerful meal. In spite of Laurel's and Rhoda's efforts to keep the talk going, there were long moments of silence. Ben never said much anyhow, and this morning Sally did not feel like joining in Nan's and Tracy's chatter. She wished they would eat their breakfasts and get on the boat and go home. Everything had been fine until they had come to spoil it.

A movement outside Benjie's window caught her attention. Someone was shaking the lilac bush, causing the chickadees and sparrows to twitter and flutter. She was almost sure, though she could not see his face, that Benjie was really watching. Something about the set of his shoulders looked alert and attentive. Nobody else noticed, and she said nothing. If they all started exclaiming or even just staring at him, he would crawl back into his shell.

The shaking of the bush grew more violent. A blue jay flew down out of nowhere and lighted on a branch, scolding furiously at something below the windowsill. Then Ree-ject came into view, clawing and scrambling frantically to reach the bird feeder. She was having a hard time. The branches of the bush were too slender to give her much support, and she kept slipping. Once she almost fell, but caught herself and hung by one paw, her eyes wide with surprise, her triangular mouth stretched in a yowl of protest. Normally so surefooted and graceful, she looked perfectly ridiculous in the awkward position.

For one crazy split second, Sally thought that she herself had laughed out loud. Then she saw the stunned faces around the table. It was Benjie who was laughing, loudly and joyously, bouncing in his chair and clapping his hands. Before anyone could move, he jumped down, raced to the door, and flung it open. By the time the rest of them had recovered, he had caught Ree-ject and was marching back into the house with her tight in his arms. His eyes sparkled and his whole face shone.

Nobody said anything for a long moment, but words were unnecessary. It was perfectly clear to everyone that Benjie was going to stay on the island.

CHAPTER 11

After Easter, winter really let go its iron grip on Star Island. The last trace of snow disappeared like magic, and the ground began to thaw under the climbing sun and the southerly breezes. Migrating birds—goldfinches, flickers, cedar waxwings, warblers—stopped to rest and feed at the island on their way north. Along the brook the alders shook out powdery catkins, and skunk cabbages reared their queer bronze helmets. The leafless rhodora blazed magenta in waste places, and under patches of pine needles shy arbutus put forth its waxy, fragrant blooms. At dusk the shrill, sweet piping of frogs drifted from the bogs. It was a lovely, awakening time of the year.

It was also a busy time. After the winter's long inactivity there was suddenly much to be done outdoors. Sally came home from school one afternoon to find Ben and Rhoda searching through the woodshed for old brooms and burlap bags. Today, they told Sally, it had been decided to burn off the barren.

"We won't get a better chance at it," Ben said.

"There's no wind to speak of, and the last year's growth has dried out enough to catch fire. You have to do these things when the time's right."

"I guess so," Sally agreed. "Or I would if I knew what you were talking about."

Ben looked surprised. Then he laughed. "I'm talking about burning the dead grass and weeds off that big blueberry field up above the village. We do it every two or three years. You have to, if you want to get any kind of a crop of blueberries."

This was news to Sally. "Can I go, too?" she asked.

It was Rhoda's turn to look surprised. "Everybody goes," she said, "from the cradle to the grave. Old Perley'll be there—you couldn't keep him away. And I'm going to take Benjie. He'll be all right, so long as I keep him close by me. Why, burning the blueberry barren is what you might call one of the big social events of the year, out here on the island. Not that we have so many, when you come right down to it, but we make the most of what we have." She laughed. "It's supposed to be men's work, and half a dozen men could do it easy. But everybody likes to play with fire, and this is a good excuse. So we all go—men, women, children, and dogs. Here, take these crocus sacks into the house and soak them in water."

A crocus sack, Sally observed, was simply a burlap bag.

When the Coopers and Sally, with Benjie in tow, arrived at the great field below the woods, they found most of the villagers already there. Everybody was armed with old brooms and wet sacks, and everybody was in high spirits. Horace Vance, the first selectman, was in charge.

"Ben, you go along to the northward there, with Lon and Perley, and get the fires started on that side," Horace ordered. "The rest of you string out along the edge of the woods, about ten feet apart. Keep a snug watch up there. We don't want no forest fire to get going."

"I'll stay down here out of the way, on account of Benjie," Rhoda said. "We'll just watch. You go along, Sally."

Sally made her way to the top of the field, where she found Linda, leaning on a broom and talking to Miss Mills. The teacher looked younger and different in slacks and a sweater. To the right and left, spaced in a thin line along the edge of the woods, were most of the women and children of the village, swinging their brooms idly, calling back and forth to each other.

"What are we supposed to do?" Sally asked Linda.

"If any little fires start along here, put them out. Whack them with your crocus sack or sweep them out with your broom. Of course"—Linda grinned a little—"they'd go out, anyhow. My father says you couldn't set the woods afire with a tanker load of kerosene, they're so wet this time of year. But it's sort of fun pretending we're saving the island."

Before Sally could answer, there was a stir along the waiting line, and Linda shouted, "Whoops, they're setting her ablaze! Spread out, spread out!" Linda enjoyed giving orders, especially to Miss Mills. This was probably the only opportunity she would ever have to do that.

Sally looked down the slope. She could see the men at the bottom of the field touching the tall dry grass at intervals with flaming torches. At first, only slim columns of smoke rose straight in the still air. Then the dead vegetation caught with a *whoosh!* and a sudden wall of fire leaped up. Quickly and steadily it started climbing the hill, crackling, sending up great swirls of orange flame, blotting out the village and the sea beyond with a thick black pall of smoke.

The crackling grew louder and the flames leaped higher as the fire created its own updraft. Now Sally could feel its heat on her face. Off to her left, Linda was shouting happily and beating the ground with her wet sack. Sally looked down and saw a small flame at her feet. She swiped at it with her broom, and it vanished as quickly as it had appeared. Then there was another and another, and she swept them away. All along the line she could hear shouting and the slap of wet sacks, but she was too busy defending her own small position to worry about anyone else.

Then, as the flames reached the damp shelter of the woods, they died down. The smoke drifted away, and the great field lay black against the blue of the sea. The excitement was over, but it had been fun while it lasted.

Late that night, Sally looked up toward the high blueberry barren and saw a few small fires burning harmlessly there. They looked strange and lovely, like new, low-hanging stars. In the morning, the field—which had been blood-red last fall, white all winter, and faded brown only yesterday—loomed like a black scar over the village. For several days everybody's outdoor clothing smelled rather pleasantly of wood-smoke.

The smoke finally aired out of jackets, and one morning the black field was faintly tinged with green, as though someone had spread a delicate veil over it. Seeing it, Rhoda made an impatient sound.

"This time of year always gives me the fidgets," she complained. "My fingers are itching to get started on my garden, but the soil's still too cold and wet for planting. Well, at least I can take the mulch off my daffodils and clean up the yard. Everything looks so shabby and neglected after the snow's gone, as though nobody gave a hoot. I'll get at it this very day."

Sure enough, when Sally came home from school, Rhoda was vigorously raking away the half-rotted seaweed and leaves that had protected her daffodil and tulip bulbs from the winter's cold. Benjie was running around the yard in pursuit of Ree-ject, who seemed to be infected with spring fever, too.

"Nothing's winter-killed, as farforth as I can see," Rhoda informed Sally contentedly. She pointed to a clump of fat green spears thrusting from the earth. "See? They're making a good thrifty start. Now if you was a-mind to get the wheelbarrow out of the shed, I can clean up this mess before supper, and tomorrow—"

Sally went for the wheelbarrow. On the way back,

acting on impulse, she scooped Benjie up, plumped him into the awkward vehicle, picked up the handles, and began walking. After a startled intake of breath, Benjie loved the ride. He clung to both sides of the barrow, laughing and crowing delightedly.

"Okay, Benjie, that's it," Sally said when she reached Rhoda. "Out you go." Everybody had acquired the habit of talking to Benjie as though he could understand. "Come on, you can help me and Rhoda pick up this mess." She began tossing handfuls of the mulch into the wheelbarrow.

To her complete surprise, Benjie followed her example.

"My—land!" Rhoda spaced the words. "Why, it almost looks like he understood you."

It did indeed. Soundlessly, busily, Benjie worked along with the other two until the wheelbarrow was full. Then Rhoda asked, her voice a little too offhand, "Want a ride, Benjie?"

Benjie looked at her. Then he scrambled into the wheelbarrow, turned around, and sat down composedly on the pile of mulch. There was no doubt about it. Benjie did understand what was said to him—understood and obeyed.

It seemed like a miracle. That was what Sally heard Rhoda tell Miss Bridges when the social worker made her May visit to the island.

Sally was not so sure. "I'll bet he understood us all along," she said, "only the little rascal was too stubborn

and ornery to let on." She said it fondly, as though admiring Benjie's strength of character, and the two women smiled.

"No," Miss Bridges told her, "that isn't true. That child was really withdrawn, really cut off from his surroundings. We'll probably never know what has made the change. The human mind is a very mysterious thing. Probably no one thing is responsible, but a combination of things." She shrugged—a gesture unlike Miss Bridges. "Perhaps it is a miracle. Let's not try to explain it. Let's just be thankful for it."

As the sun rose higher in the heavens each day, and the earth became warmer, all the women of the island spent their afternoons working in their dooryards. When she left the school, Sally could see them, each busy in her own domain, raking, spading, calling back and forth to each other in the bright, windy sunshine. With their faces flushed, their sleeves rolled up, and their skirts blowing in the fitful breezes, they all looked younger and prettier than they had in winter. It was rather like the burning of the barren—something that was a part of a Star Island spring. Although each worked alone, still they all seemed to be working together.

One afternoon, as Sally and Linda were walking up the road, Lavina Wells stopped them. "Ask your mother," she said to Linda, "and you ask Rhoda, Sally, if either of them want any dahlia bulbs. I've got more than I can use here. They multiplied like Tophet last year. I had some real unusual ones. They came from Harvey's cousin over on the main. Rhoda'll remember. She admired them last fall."

Rhoda remembered. "I was casting asparagus eyes at them dahlias of Lavina's all summer long, hoping she'd offer. You change out of your school clothes quick, Sally, and run down and fetch them before she has time to change her mind. Here, Benjie, pick up all them twigs and put them in the wheelbarrow." Benjie worked with Rhoda every afternoon, silent and busy, almost a real help. "Then I'll give you a ride to the trash heap." She added to Sally, "I don't know whether he'd do it without the promise of a ride or not, and I'm taking no chances. Well, go on. Change your clothes and hightail it down to Lavina's."

But when Sally came out of the house, Lavina was in the yard with a basket full of bulbs on her hip. "I thought I might as well bring them up myself—take what they call a coffee break over on the main." She set the basket down and looked around her. "You're making real progress here— Rhoda, can that be *Benjie*?" She knew very well that it was. "Why, I hadn't realized! I haven't seen him to pay attention to him for quite a spell, and he acts like a different child. Maybe he's got his feet braced at last. Some young ones are slow starters, and in the end they like as not outrun the others. Benjie may be that kind."

Rhoda said cautiously, "He's improving all the time.

I'm half scared to hope for too much, but he's improving."

"I should say he is!" Lavina fell into thought, watching Benjie trying to move the wheelbarrow. Then she said, "Billy's old tricycle's somewhere out amongst the cultch in our shed. He's outgrown it. He's eight now, and all he thinks of is boats. I'll have him root it out—the tricycle, I mean—if you think Benjie—"

"That's real thoughtful of you, Lavina," Rhoda said sincerely. "It's worth a try, at least, and I do thank you."

Benjie took to the tricycle like a duck to water. For a few days he rode it round and round the dooryard, falling off occasionally and running into things once in a while, but becoming more expert all the time. Then one morning during spelling, Sally glanced out the schoolhouse window and saw Benjie sailing down the middle of the road.

For a startled instant she thought that the tricycle had run away with him, but immediately Rhoda came into view, walking unconcernedly, evidently on her way to the store. They looked, Sally thought, like any ordinary grandmother and grandchild doing an errand together. Seeing them, nobody would guess that Benjie was not quite—well, ordinary.

When she went home that noon for dinner, she said to Rhoda, "I saw you and Benjie sashaying down the road this morning like the white hen and her chick. I just wish Nathan and Laurel could have seen you. Then I guess there wouldn't have been any more talk about that darned school."

Rhoda drew a deep breath, let it out, and laughed. "That was a close call, all right, back Eastertime. But Benjie's come a long way since then, and an awful long way since he first came here. Next time his folks visit us, I don't believe he'll cut up the didoes he did last time. He'll be all over his shyness of other people by then, at the rate he's going."

"At the rate he's going—" Sally began, and then stopped short. There was no danger now of Benjie's being taken away and put into a special school—of that she was sure. But, at the rate he was going, didn't another danger loom—one she had not thought of before?

"Cat got your tongue?" Rhoda asked.

"No. Only—Rhoda, suppose Benjie gets to be like other boys his age, just an ordinary four-year-old kid? What's going to happen then?"

Rhoda understood at once. "It's something I try not to think about. If— Not *if*. *When*," she amended fiercely. "*When* Benjie can cope with things like an ordinary young one, his rightful place is with his own family. He's theirs, and they can give him advantages that we can't. I just try not to look that far ahead, though of course the day will come—"

"He belongs here," Sally interrupted hotly. "Advantages! Look how he's changed since he's been here. Isn't that the biggest advantage he could have? They didn't give it to him. We did."

Rhoda shook her head. "We have to be fair. Maybe this would have happened anyhow, wherever he was. Who knows? And he is their son."

"He can't go. Tracy and Nan— Rhoda, they don't even like him. You ought to hear the way they talk about him, and see how they act with him. He needs *us*."

She meant, "He needs me, instead of those silly sisters of his." She understood him, she needed him— That was it. Nobody ever before had depended on her as Benjie did, had ever given her that warm, wordless feeling deep inside of being needed. From the time when she was very small, she had always been independent Sally Gray, who went her own way, who really cared for nobody, who was free as a bird from any ties. Now she was no longer free. She was bound to Benjie. She needed him as much as he needed her.

Seeing her face, Rhoda said gently, "Let's take one day at a time, Sally. Benjie still has lots to learn."

Yes, he had to learn to talk, to think for himself, to take care of himself in all sorts of situations. She hoped it would be a long, long time before—

Sally pulled her thoughts up sharply, horrified at herself. She had almost wished that Benjie wouldn't get any better. Even half wishing that was the most terrible thing she had ever done.

She said quickly, "I want Benjie to get well more than anything in the world." She wanted to make that clear to herself even more than to Rhoda. "I'd give anything, do anything— I'd cut off my hair, if it would help Benjie any."

Rhoda laughed spontaneously. She knew exactly how much Sally's braids meant to her. "I believe you would, at that," she said. In an unusual gesture of affection she put her arm around Sally. "Did anyone ever tell you that you're a nice kid?" she asked.

CHAPTER 12

Spring was rushing toward summer. Suddenly it was almost June. Along the edge of the woods, sugar pear and rowan trees shook out their lacy blossoms. They looked like tall angels in flowing white robes against the dark evergreens. Beneath the low blueberry bushes the barren was carpeted with short-stemmed purple violets. Along the shore, goose grass and goldthread pushed bravely out of crevices in the rocks. The gulls became very busy and officious, building their nests on bleak offshore reefs and fighting each other more viciously than ever in defense of them. In village gardens, daffodils tossed their golden heads in the wind, and peonies budded. Robins hopped about the tiny lawns crowded between outcropping ledges, cocking their heads as they listened for earthworms. The lilacs were great mounds of lavender and white bloom. Their fragrance drifted in at windows that had been closed all winter but were now open to the soft salt air.

The changing season affected the people as well as the land, filling them with new energy. Now the sun rose very early and set late, and the long daylight hours were full of activity. The men set out more lobster traps than before, ranging far on the broad pastures of the sea in search of good fishing grounds. During their time ashore they painted their boats and the trim of their houses. The women plunged into housecleaning, washing windows, scrubbing woodwork, beating rugs, and hanging blankets out to sun and air.

Miss Mills turned into a slave driver. With only a few weeks left to accomplish it, she was determined that her pupils should be perfect in everything before she left for the long summer vacation. Sally had less time to gaze out the windows these days. When she did raise her eyes from her books, she often saw Benjie pedaling his tricycle along the road or playing with the Chandlers' dog or dragging Ree-ject around in a little cart that Ben had made for him.

Benjie, she thought fondly, was getting pretty independent. He amused himself very well, all things considered. Rhoda kept an eye on him, of course, but she was leaving him more and more to his own devices. With her housecleaning and gardening, she was in and out of the house constantly, and she no longer felt it necessary to take him with her every time she went inside to baste a roast or get another basket of laundry. Remembering Rhoda's hovering concern and Benjie's wooden unresponsiveness when he had first come to the island, Sally realized afresh how much they both had changed in the past months. Then Benjie had not seemed to hear when he was spoken to. Now he not only heard, but he came when called, and carried out simple directions. He recognized his own name and the names of those around him, and the names of common objects like chairs and cups and jackets. Benjie, like everything else on the island, seemed to be awakening from a long winter's sleep.

One morning, Miss Mills announced a surprise grammar test for the older children. This was greeted with subdued groans.

"That's enough of that," Miss Mills said sharply. "Year after next, some of you will be going over to Stillport to high school, and I fully intend that you'll go well prepared. I'm not going to have it said that pupils from one-room schools, and this one-room school in particular, are not properly trained. You're going to be well grounded in the fundamentals—that I promise you. So sharpen your pencils and your wits, and we'll get to work."

She started writing on the blackboard, and soon the room was quiet except for the rustle of papers and the sounds that drifted in through the open windows—the familiar, unheeded mewing of gulls, the rumble of surf, and the occasional distant voices of the island women. When Miss Mills used her sharp tone, everybody knew that it was no time for nonsense.

Sally was making a difficult choice between *lay* and *lie* when the quiet was shattered. First there was the quick, loud pounding of feet on the schoolhouse steps, and then the door banged open. Rhoda stood in the doorway. Her face was worried, but she spoke calmly.

"Miss Mills, I'm sorry to interrupt, but Benjie's missing. We—the other women and I—can't find him anywhere. I just went into the house for a minute, and when I came out, he was gone." Her voice rose dangerously. "If any harm's come to him—" With an effort, she controlled herself. "The men are all out hauling, except for Perley and Bert Elder, so I didn't know where else to turn but here."

Miss Mills understood at once. "Of course, Mrs. Cooper. We'll all help find him. He can't have gone far." She clapped her hands. "School is dismissed, children. File out in an ordinary manner and wait for me in the yard. Leave your test papers on my desk as you go."

Sally was already at Rhoda's side. "Where did you see him last, Rhoda? What was he doing? Where have you looked?"

"Everywhere. All through the village. Oh, I don't know!" Her voice trembled. "He was right there, Sally, right in the yard, playing with some sticks and pebbles, as good as gold, and then he was gone. He didn't take his tricycle. If anything's happened to him—" She went quickly out of the school and started up the road, almost running.

If anything had happened to Benjie! Sally refused to face the thought. No harm could come to him—not on the island. It was safe here. There were no cars, no cruel, wicked people, no vicious animals. What possible trouble could a child get into on the island?

As though in answer to the unspoken question, Rhoda said, "Supposing he's fallen into the sea? Oh, Sally, I keep thinking that! He couldn't holler for help, like most young ones. He'd just—"

"Stop that!" Sally couldn't bear to hear the word "drown." She drew a quick, painful breath, seeing Benjie—poor, speechless little Benjie—struggling silently in the icy green water. "He hasn't fallen in. Somebody would have seen him—Perley or Bert or one of the women—if he went down along the harbor. He hasn't had time to get to the other shores. Rhoda, he's all right."

"If he was like other kids— My own I never worried about. I knew they could take care of themselves. But Benjie can't, Sally. For all he's four years old and big for his age, in most things he's still a baby. Oh, I should never have left him. I should never have taken my eyes off him, not for a minute."

Rhoda was getting herself all worked up, to use the island phrase for "hysterical." Sally knew how she felt. She was a little worked up herself. She wished Ben were here to take charge.

Emma Chandler and some of the other women joined them. "He's not here in the village nor down along the harbor," Emma stated positively. "He's wandered farther afield. Miss Mills has got the children organized to comb through the woods, and some of us will work along the north shore." There was something reassuring about her steady, reasonable voice and manner. "Rhoda, maybe you'd better stay here in case he comes home of his own accord."

"I can't," Rhoda protested quickly. "I'd go crazy, just waiting. I've got to be doing something." •

Emma nodded sympathetically. "I'll stay, then. In case he shows up, I'll ring the school bell. A day like this, it'll be heard all over the island. You and Sally go along the south shore. That way, the whole island will be covered." She put a work-worn hand on Rhoda's shoulder. "Don't fret. We'll find him safe as houses."

Rhoda tried valiantly to smile. "If he could only answer. But call his name, anyhow. Benjie don't answer, but he comes when he's called." She added a bit bleakly, "That is, if he's able, if he's not—"

"Now don't go borrowing trouble," Emma commanded, and made a shooing motion with her apron. Obediently the little group broke up and moved away. Their voices, calling "Benjie, Be-e-enji-ie," came back, diminishing in the distance.

Sally and Rhoda cut through the Vance's apple orchard and made their way to the southerly side of the island. Although this shore was not far from the village, people seldom visited it except in autumn, to rake the wild cranberries that covered the rough ground. There was nothing else over here but wild roses, stunted fir trees, and sheltered little beaches with water too cold for swimming. Today, in the warm, bright sunshine, the whole length of shore was clearly visible against the sparkling sea. There was no sign of life anywhere, aside from spiraling gulls and one lone blue heron standing sentinel in the top of a tall dead pine.

Rhoda said despairingly, "We've got to look everywhere—behind every bush and rock, in every little cove—" She cupped her hands around her lips. "Benjie!" she called. "Be-enji-ie!" The freshening breeze snatched her voice away and lost it.

It seemed hopeless to Sally. There was so much space, and Benjie was so small. Besides, he had never in the world come over here by himself. There was no path to lead here, and no reason why he should wander in this direction. She and Rhoda were wasting time—good time that would be better spent searching more likely places.

But she could not say this to Rhoda. Rhoda was worried enough already. There was no sense in upsetting her more. Others were searching the other areas. She and Rhoda had been assigned this section, and they had better make a good thorough job of it, for their own peace of mind if for no other reason.

"Benjie!" she shouted. "Be-enji-ie!" The gulls squalled indignantly, but nothing else happened.

"We'd better go about this systematically," Rhoda said with a newfound composure. Rhoda could be pretty good at self-control. "You go along the edge of the woods, and I'll take the shore. He can't have gone too terribly far in this length of time."

"All right," Sally agreed. "If he's here, we'll find him."

🌿 133

She started zigzagging back and forth, in and out of the shadow of the trees, calling Benjie's name. Occasionally she saw Rhoda's head, bobbing up and down among the ledges and rugosa rosebushes, and once in a while she heard her voice. It was hard to distinguish it from the crying of the gulls. The human voice did not amount to much here. It was quickly lost among the natural sounds of wind and sea and birds. But of course she and Rhoda had to keep calling. Benjie might hear.

Time went on—a long time, it seemed, although when Sally paused for a moment to catch her breath and inspect some brier scratches on her legs, she saw that she and Rhoda had not come very far. The sun was still climbing, so it was not yet noon. She rubbed her scratches impatiently and started along the woods again.

Then she stopped short. There, outlined in a patch of damp earth in the shade of a tamarack tree, was a small footprint. For an instant she could not believe her eyes. She closed them tightly. When she opened them, the

footprint was still there, fresh and clear. It had to be Benjie's.

"Rhoda," she shouted, her voice coming out high and squeaky. She tried again. "Rhoda! Here, here!"

Rhoda's head turned in her direction, and as Sally waved and beckoned wildly, she scrambled up the ledges and stumbled toward her over the rough ground. Her expression was a mixture of hope and fear.

❦ 135

"He's been here!" Sally pointed to the footprint. "He was right here, not very long ago."

Rhoda stooped and touched the footprint gently with her hand, as though she had to be sure it was really there. "Benjie," she said, almost whispering. She straightened. "Oh, thank God. He can't be far—"

Then they saw him. He was trudging toward them in the sun-dappled shade of the trees, Ree-ject draped over his arm. He had not yet seen them, but he looked neither lost nor forlorn. He looked as though he knew exactly where he was and where he was going. He looked like a little boy absorbed in business of his own.

Sally's whole heart leaped out to meet him as she took a step forward, his name on her lips. Rhoda's hand closed over her arm in a painful grip, and Sally turned in protest.

"Don't," Rhoda said urgently. "Let's not startle him. He's all right. Let's not make a big catouse."

Sally looked at her with respect. She knew exactly how much Rhoda wanted to fling herself on Benjie, gathering him in her arms, exclaiming over him, maybe crying, perhaps even scolding him a little. She knew, because that was what she herself wanted to do. And she would have, too, but for Rhoda. She hadn't Rhoda's self-discipline or the wisdom that placed Benjie's good above her own feelings. She had a lot to learn yet from Rhoda, she thought humbly.

Now Benjie caught sight of them and his face broke into a wide smile.

"Hi there, Benjie." Rhoda was quiet and casual. "What are you doing here?"

"Ree-ject ran away," Benjie announced clearly, "but I caught her."

For a moment Sally thought she was dreaming. This could not possibly be happening. In a minute she would wake up. Rhoda's suddenly white face brought her back to reality.

"That's good." Rhoda's voice was almost steady. "It's most dinnertime, Benjie. We'd better be getting on home."

Benjie shifted Ree-ject from his arm to his shoulder. "Okay," he agreed cheerfully, as though he had been talking all his life.

Sally found her tongue. "I—I—Rhoda—I—Benjie—" Words failed her again.

The color was coming back into Rhoda's face, and her smile was beautiful. "I know, Sally. I feel the same way." She looked down at Benjie, and the look said everything that words could not.

"Oh!" Sally suddenly remembered. "The others are still out looking. Maybe I'd better—"

"Yes. Run as fast as you can and ring the school bell. That'll let them know. Benjie and I'll be right along." She touched his hair. "Won't we, Benjie?"

"Ree-ject, too," Benjie corrected.

There was no one in sight when Sally burst out of the Vance's orchard. She flew down the empty road to the deserted schoolhouse, tore open the door, seized the dangling bell rope, and pulled with all her might. Above her, in the little cupola, the bell jangled crazily. Then, as she caught the right rhythm, its harsh, sweet clamor rang out over the whole island.

Everybody would hear it, she thought. Wherever they were—in the woods, on the barren, along the shore, clean over to the Backside—people would stop and listen and know that Benjie had been found.

Rhoda would hear it, too. But to her the wild and joyous pealing would have a different meaning. It would be a celebration. Benjie at last had broken his silence. Benjie could talk!

CHAPTER 13

The last two weeks of school passed like a dream as far as Sally was concerned. She was present every day. She answered Miss Mills's questions more or less correctly, and safely passed all the year-end examinations. She did her part of the housework that Miss Mills insisted they all share. But always in the back of her mind was the thought of Benjie and the wonderful thing that had happened to him. She raced home from school each day just to hear him chatter.

For chatter Benjie did. As Rhoda said, "Now that he's discovered the gift of gab, it seems like he's making up for lost time." She listened to Benjie's voice running on in a one-sided conversation with Ree-ject. "That's the sweetest sound I ever heard in all my born days. Sometimes, Sally, I can't really believe I'm hearing it."

Sally agreed with her thoroughly. She had never thought to wonder how Benjie would sound, if ever he spoke—whether his voice would be soft or shrill or perhaps rusty with disuse. Now that she at last heard it, she would not have been able to describe it. It was, as

Rhoda said, simply the sweetest sound she had ever heard. It sounded just like Benjie.

Rhoda and Ben and Sally were not the only ones to rejoice. During the two weeks after Benjie had followed Ree-ject over onto the south shore and found his tongue, everybody on the island made opportunities to talk to him. They clustered around him when Rhoda took him to the store, or stopped him as he rode his tricycle along the road, or paused by the Coopers' yard where he was playing to say, "Hello, Benjie. How are you today?"

"I'm okay, Grandma's okay, Grandpa's okay, Ree-ject's okay," Benjie would tell them. "Sally's gone to school." They would laugh delightedly.

"Don't that beat all?" they would ask each other; and they would walk on, smiling. There were so few people on the island, and they knew each other so well, that what happened to one of them was important to all of them.

Rhoda said, though, "I'll be glad when this nine days' wonder dies down and folks stop making such a to-do about Benjie. Elsewise, first thing we know, we're going to have one spoiled young one on our hands."

Perhaps she was right, Sally thought, but maybe Benjie had a little spoiling coming to him to make up for everything he had missed.

That very first day of Benjie's talking, Rhoda had wanted Ben to go over to Stillport immediately to telephone Nathan and Laurel the marvelous news. "They're his parents. They deserve to know right away," she had said.

Ben was doubtful. "We don't know if it's going to last. They'd come rushing down this very weekend, and what if he acted like he did last time? Better wait a while."

"It don't seem fair." Rhoda thought a minute. "Soon as school is closed, they're coming for a visit, and it don't seem right that they should be unprepared. At least I ought to write them."

"You do that. You write them. A letter ain't so upsetting as a phone call. And don't go overboard, Rhody. Don't make it sound like Benjie's ready to give the commencement speech up to Orono." The state university was in Orono. "Just take it kind of easy, will you?"

"Now, Ben Cooper," Rhoda began indignantly, "when did I ever go overboard about—?" She met his amused eye. "Well, maybe, once in a dog's age. But this time I'll be careful. I'll just say that we *think*, maybe—perhaps—God willing and the creek don't rise, Benjie might possibly be getting ready to say a word or two. Does that suit you?"

Ben laughed and spanked her lightly. "That suits me fine."

Sally had not seen them fool around like that since way back before Rhoda's birthday, and it seemed good.

On the last day of school there were no lessons. Miss Mills was to leave on the afternoon ferry for the summer, so there was only one session. This was to take the form of a Visiting Day for everyone on the island, followed by a picnic in the Vance's orchard, a site chosen because it was nearby.

The guests arrived promptly at half-past ten, the appointed time. Tom Smith, because he was the oldest pupil by a few weeks, made a little speech of welcome and invited everyone to inspect the drawings and papers that Miss Mills had scotch-taped to the blackboards. Sally was pleased to find that one of her arithmetic exercises and a composition she had written about the surf on the Backside were among the items on display.

Then Miss Mills awarded the prize for the best bird list. She said that in a way everybody had won a prize, because everybody had gained both pleasure and knowledge from the bird-feeding project. Since Linda had the longest and neatest list of birds observed, she won an extra prize, an illustrated field guide to the birds. Sally was pleased. Linda had really wanted to win, and had worked long and hard to do so.

Horace Vance, the first selectman, made a speech thanking Miss Mills for the good job she had done as schoolteacher, and led the assembly in singing "For She's a Jolly Good Fellow." Miss Mills turned pink with pleasure and said that she was the one who should be extending thanks for all the kindnesses shown her by the people of Star Island. "And now," she concluded, when Horace showed signs of making still another speech, "it's time we adjourned to the orchard for our picnic."

Everyone had brought lunches from home, and Miss Mills contributed cases of soda pop. The pupils were responsible for the dessert. Sally and Linda had spent the evening before in making an enormous chocolate cake, refusing help or advice from anyone. It sagged a little in the middle, but they filled the hollow with extra-thick frosting, assuring each other that nobody would notice. Anyhow, they quoted wisely, the proof of the cake was in the eating, and this one sure tasted good. Old Perley Stevens, Sally was glad to see, had brought a big bagful of his famous hermits as his donation, and several of the men carried buckets full of boiled lobsters, which were almost as delicious cold, with bread-and-butter sandwiches, as they were hot. Nobody was going hungry on this picnic, that was certain.

The group straggled up the hill to the orchard and sat down on the dry grass under the flowering trees. It really was nice here, Sally thought, looking around. The sunlight sifted down through the branches, and the air was full of the scent of apple blossoms and the sound of bees busy among the flowers overhead. A warm breeze blew fitfully, shaking down handfuls of petals in a slow, gentle rain. It could not have been a better day for a picnic if she herself had made it to order, she decided. She dropped down cross-legged beside Rhoda, Benjie, and Ben.

"Hi there, Benjie." Perley lowered his lank frame onto the grass beside Benjie. "How's old Ree-ject making out?"

"She caught a mouse," Benjie reported.

"I wouldn't be one mite surprised. All Samanthy's kittens make top-notch mousers. Always have. Like their mother." Samantha, in Perley's mind, was a cat without equal.

Rhoda leaned forward to say, "Perley, I don't know as I ever thanked you for that kitten. She's no great shakes for looks, but I do believe it's largely her we have to thank for Benjie's getting well. The store he sets by her!"

"It probably would have happened anyhow," Perley assured her carelessly, but it was easy to see that he was pleased. "If Ree-ject gave him a shove in the right direction, that's good, but I don't know as I'd give her all the credit. Lots of other things entered in—"

He broke off to accept from Emma Chandler a plate piled high with sandwiches, a deviled egg, a stuffed tomato, and a large lobster. By common consent she was overseeing the distribution of the food. "Thanks, Emma. I'm a good cook myself, I don't mind saying, but it's a treat to taste someone else's victuals."

Everybody else apparently felt the same way, and for a while there was very little conversation. Then Miss Mills beckoned to Sally and Linda. "Some of our guests are ready for dessert, girls," she said. "If you'll just supervise the smaller children?"

Until now, Benjie had sat quietly, eating his lunch and talking with Perley. But when he saw Billy and Jenny and Ray, who were not much larger than he, passing plates of cookies and cake, it was too much for him.

He scrambled up and ran to Miss Mills.

"I'll help, too," he said.

She smiled. "Good. We can use all the help we can get. Show him what to do, Sally."

Sally gave him a plate of cupcakes and told him to be sure that everybody got one. "And when people say 'Thank you,' be sure to say 'You're welcome,' Benjie," she instructed him.

She kept an eye on him, smiling to see how serious and careful he was with his plate of cakes, and how faithful with his You're welcome's. Darling Benjie! He did just as well as anybody in the whole school.

Finally Miss Mills looked at her watch. "It's too bad we have to end this happy time," she called out, "but the ferry's about due. This won't be good-bye," she added. "I'll be back in September, and we'll go right on where we've left off. Except"—she smiled at Benjie—"it looks as though I'll have one more pupil then."

Everybody clapped at that idea, and then it was time to escort Miss Mills down to the landing, with the men carrying her luggage, and the children jostling for the honor of walking next to her. They all liked Miss Mills, even if she was a teacher with peculiar ideas sometimes.

Although, Sally thought, that idea about Benjie's going to school next year wasn't peculiar. It was good. Benjie could do the work, she'd bet, if— She sighed. It was a big *if*. He might not even be here next year.

❧ 146

The Nathan Coopers arrived from Boston two weeks later. They were going to stay a month. Rhoda was full of plans for picnics and clam-digging expeditions and excursions to uninhabited outlying islands. She told Sally that she was going to make islanders out of Tracy and Nan if it was the last thing she ever did in this world.

"I've about given up on Laurel," she admitted. "I didn't get hold of her young enough. But the girls— Well, look at you. It didn't take you long to fall into our ways."

Sally had to agree. She felt completely at home on the island and loved everything about it dearly. Maybe, in a month, Tracy and Nan would begin to feel the same way. It wouldn't surprise her a bit.

Much of the two weeks was spent in trying to prepare Benjie for the coming visit. Sally and Rhoda told him again and again who was coming, and he repeated the names faithfully, and seemed to understand. When Linda popped in on Friday and suddenly asked, "Who's coming tomorrow, Benjie?" he answered promptly, "Mommy and Daddy and Tracy and Nan."

"See?" Linda said triumphantly. "He knows. You know, don't you, Benjie?"

"Sure, I know," Benjie agreed, as he scooped Ree-ject up and started out the door.

"I'm not so sure." Rhoda sounded worried. "He

sounds like he does, but there's no telling how he'll act with strangers when he's face to face with them."

"You can't call his own family exactly strangers," Linda objected.

"How do we know? We don't know how much he remembers from before he got better. We don't know if he remembers anything or anybody at all. Likely we never will know."

"He'll soon get used to them, even if he doesn't remember them," Sally volunteered. "Benjie learns awful fast nowadays."

She said it again the next morning as she and Rhoda and Benjie waited on the landing for Ben's boat to come into sight from the mainland.

"Yes," Rhoda conceded, "but remember last time? He's comfortable as an old shoe with us on the island, but with strangers—I'm hoping—"

It was clear what Rhoda was hoping, Sally thought: that Benjie would not be frightened by the new faces. But what did she herself hope?

She looked at Benjie, tossing little chips of wood off the wharf and screaming excitedly as the small harbor pollack rose from the shadowy water and snatched them. Ree-ject was twining herself in and out between his feet, and he was trying to make her look at the fish. His face shone, his eyes sparkled, even his dark hair seemed charged with life. He was being noisy and boisterous and bossy and altogether unreasonable with Ree-ject. He was almost being a brat. Sally's whole heart went out to him, and she knew what she hoped.

She loved him and she didn't want him to leave her and the island for years and years and years, but she had to hope that he'd go on acting just like this while his mother and father and sisters were here. It might mean losing him almost at once, but she couldn't hope for anything else. She couldn't wish for a return, even for a moment, of the dull-eyed, voiceless puppet that had been Benjie.

"If he keeps on like this," she asked, "do you think they'll want to take him with them when they go?"

"We'll see," Rhoda said placidly. When Rhoda said "We'll see," it usually meant that she was going to see that things went her way. "I imagine I can persuade Nathan to leave him here with us for another year or so. Benjie has just about got used to things here. I doubt if he's ready to tackle a new place."

"Not until he's better adjusted," Sally said blandly, using Miss Bridges' word.

Rhoda slanted amused eyes at her. "And feels more secure," she said, poker-faced. "Those are two good words to use on Nathan. They sound like something they'd say at that danged school. Thank you for reminding me, Sally. And speaking of school, Benjie'll be able to go, here on the island. I'll mention that to Nathan, too. Benjie'd be too young, over on the main. They've got rules about age, over there. I suppose we've got the same rules here, if we care to think about it. But out here, rules are bendable. Nobody's going to raise a ruckus here about Benjie's being underage."

That was true, Sally knew. She also knew that Rhoda was going to win any argument she might have with Nathan and Laurel over Benjie's staying a little longer on the island. She had her winning look about her.

"I know he can't stay here forever," Sally said slowly. "I know he has to leave. But it seems like we've just found him, really. It's too soon for us to have to let him go."

Rhoda nodded. "I know. I felt the same way when each one of my three boys left home. It was too soon— but they went anyhow. That's part of life, I guess—seeing the people you care about go their own ways, learning to let them go without too much fuss."

Sally thought about it. She had seen plenty of people come and go in her life, but not since she could remember had she cared much one way or the other. Not until now.

"I don't know what I'm going to do without Benjie," she said. "Even if he doesn't go for another year, I don't know how I'm going to get along without him."

Rhoda nodded. "I felt the same way when Steve joined the Navy. He was the youngest and the last to leave home, and his going left an awful empty place. I didn't know how I was going to get along, either."

"How did you?"

"Oh, someone always comes along to fill the hole in

your life. Though sometimes you have to go look for that someone"—she touched Sally's arm gently—"like Ben and me looked for you and found you, Sally."

Benjie tugged at their clothing. "Hey, here comes Grandpa's boat! Hey, Ree-ject, see the boat!" He began to jump up and down. "Company's coming. I see the company. I see Mommy and Daddy!"

Rhoda and Sally exchanged glances over his head. Benjie would be all right. What had they been worrying about?

Benjie started spinning around and around like a top and emitting earsplitting squeals. Then he picked up a large stone and threw it into the water. Rhoda stepped back just too late to avoid the splash, and dabbed disgustedly at the wet front of her freshly laundered dress. She regarded Benjie thoughtfully through narrowed eyes.

"That young man," she stated with complete detachment, "is building up to getting his britches warmed for him. Maybe not today or tomorrow or even next month, but sooner or later, I'll guarantee to give him the spanking he's begging for."

Sally whooped. Spank Benjie—poor little frightened, backward Benjie? Suddenly she felt wonderful. Benjie was going to be more than all right. He was going to be fine. Sometime in the foreseeable future he was going to get his britches warmed, just like any other normal little boy.

❧ 151